ME, MYSELF AND WHY?

MaryJanice Davidson

ME, MYSELF AND WHY?

ST. MARTIN'S PRESS
NEW YORK

This is a work of fiction. All of the characters, organizations, and events portrayed in this novel are either products of the author's imagination or are used fictitiously.

www.stmartins.com

Book design by Elina D. Nudelman

ISBN 978-0-312-53117-1

First Edition: October 2010

10 9 8 7 6 5 4 3 2 1

For my husband, who tries so very hard to make me stick to a daily schedule. Strictly for my own good, of course, and not because he's insanely jealous that I get to sleep whenever I want. Love you, sweetie!

Acknowledgments

First, a thousand thank-yous to my ridiculously supportive editor, Monique Patterson at St. Martin's Press. When I thought up a trilogy about an FBI agent with multiple personality disorder, I wasn't sure anyone would go for it. The truth is, this book presented challenges I'd never faced before.

However, though I was cringing like a craven dog at the task before me, Monique was nothing but enthusiastic and fearless, from my casual "what if?" pitch over burritos and throughout the writing and editing process. Monique's faith never wavered. This was comforting, if terrifying.

My agent, Ethan Ellenberg, who worked hard on a deal for the Me, Myself and Why? trilogy, and never complains when I consistently lose paperwork. You know how some people believe everyone's hell is individual? My hell will be to be reincarnated as Ethan's assistant and forced to deal with authors like me. Memo to me: Embrace the horror.

Thanks are also due to my father, Alexander Davidson, who was a terrific sounding board when I was trying to figure out when to sign on the dotted line, and gave me much valuable advice during contract negotiations.

Special thanks for my dear friends Cathie and Stacy, who love me enough to worry about me when I get jammed up with deadlines and forget to e-mail back . . . and I'm even more grateful for their patience when I disappear from the online world. They are much better friends to me than I am to them.

Speaking of disappearing from the online world, thanks are also due to my Yahoo! group, who are very patient when I don't post for weeks on end. They are the friendliest, least flaming-est group on the Web; you can check them out at http://groups.yahoo.com/group/maryjanice/.

Thanks to my sister, Yvonne, who always stops what she's doing on a business trip to call and tell me which airport is carrying my books.

Thanks to my mother, who forces my books on her unsuspecting colleagues at various antique shows.

And thanks, always, to the readers, who don't mind following me down the occasional strange path.

Author's Note

In the real world, the FBI tends to screen out mentally disturbed applicants (at least, that's their official stance). Also, there aren't nearly as many serial killers out there as the movies (and perhaps this book) would have you believe.

Also, the psychiatric community, as well as its bible, the *Diagnostic and Statistical Manual of Mental Disorders-IV* (aka the DSMMD-IV—nothing like a catchy, yet puzzling, acronym), has reclassified multiple personality disorder as dissociative identity disorder. I use the former wording for its familiarity to most readers.

A few things in this book remain true, however. Grown women do occasionally lick mirrors to turn on their partners, partners who work together can begin to resemble each other, rushed federal agents park government-issue sedans on public sidewalks, baking is lucrative, and it's possible to wake up on a Monday morning with no memory of Sunday night.

So don't say I didn't warn you.

Multiple personality disorder (MPD) is a psychiatric disorder characterized by having at least one "alter" personality that controls behavior. The "alters" are said to occur spontaneously and involuntarily, and function more or less independently of each other. The unity of consciousness, by which we identify our selves, is said to be absent in MPD. Another symptom of MPD is significant amnesia which can't be explained by ordinary forgetfulness.

—*THE SKEPTIC'S DICTIONARY*

Part of being sane is being a little bit crazy.

—JANET LONG

Here's to the crazy ones, the misfits, the rebels, the troublemakers, the round pegs in the square holes . . . the ones who see things differently—they're not fond of rules. You can quote them, disagree with them, glorify or vilify them, but the only thing you can't do is ignore them, because they change things.

—STEVE JOBS

Prologue

First comes the blood

And then comes the

First comes the blood

And then comes the

Screams, then comes the screams,
then comes the screams, and
The wheels on the bus go round and round,
Round and round,
It's so loud.
I just want to sleep, and the screams come around,
Alllll the daaaaay looooooong.
And I just want to leave, and disappear,
Disappear
Disappear
I just want to leave
And third comes the geese, alllll daaay loooong.
Are the geese really third, did they come third,
Really come third,

Or were they first?
I just want to leave, and disappear,
Alllllll geeeeeeese loooooong.
The screams won't find me, round and round,
Never will, round and round,
No they won't they never will,
Say goooood-byyyyyye.

Chapter One

The lilting strains of thrash metal crashed through my skull and I sat bolt upright in bed, clutching my ears. Someone—probably my psycho sister—had set my alarm to WROX and cranked it. It was a lot like being awakened on an airport runway by an approaching DC-10.

I clawed for the snooze button, missed, swiped again, knocked the radio to the carpet, slithered off the bed, fell on *top* of the snooze button, and, mercifully, the Sweet Jerkoffs' new release, *Raining Hell on Your Stupid Face,* stopped.

Don't ask me how I knew the song and the band. I won't tell.

"Too early," came a sonorous voice from the bed above. *What* the—? "Sleep more."

I cautiously peeked over the edge of the bed. A strange, nude man was tangled up in my Laura Ashley sheets. His long dark hair covered half his face and fluttered as he resumed snoring. He had a tattoo of Donald Duck performing a sexual act on Daisy; it was almost four inches across!

And—*what* the—?—I was naked, too.

Over his slurred protests (he smelled like he'd fallen into a tequila vat on the way to my apartment), I pulled him out of bed as efficiently and politely as I could. I found his jeans under the bed, his shirt hanging over my bedside lamp, his boxer briefs on top of the heating vent, one of his shoes in the bathroom, and the other in my kitchen sink. It was tough work getting him dressed while *not* looking at his penis, but I managed.

Don't ask me how; I won't tell.

After the stranger was gone, I set about cleaning up the empty tequila bottles, the gnawed lemon slices (one was nestled beside my toothbrush like a bedraggled yellow comma), the spilled salt shakers (my moo cow shaker! in the toilet! darn it all!), and something that looked like a small purple whale.

I was studying it, hoping it wasn't what I knew it was, when it started to buzz in my hand and I dropped it. What was *that* doing in the fridge?

Never mind. Never mind. I—I had to get to work. Mustn't be late! Mustn't be late!

I kicked the vibrator across the kitchen floor until it was close to the garbage, then darted into the bathroom. I took a quick shower, dried at light speed (my blond hair looked all right, but my eyes were bloodshot—what *had* my sister been—never mind, never mind), and dressed in my best conservative navy suit.

Then I grabbed a breakfast Hot Pocket (ham & cheese) and headed out the front door. I had a splitting headache, but some iced coffee ought to fix that nicely . . . along with about ten

Advils. No time for makeup, but I twisted my hair up into a large barrette.

"Morning, Ms. Jones," Ben, the doorman, said on my way out. "Late night, huh?"

I had no idea what he was talking about, as my last memory was of walking down Lake Street at 5:30 p.m. the day before (a peek at the newspaper assured me of the date), but nodded and waved my Hot Pocket at him.

It took ten minutes to find my Mitsubishi Eclipse—I was thankful it hadn't been towed again, intruding crookedly on the sidewalk as it was—and another twenty-five to drive (a bit more quickly than usual) to BOFFO headquarters, located on Marquette Avenue in Minneapolis. It looked like an office building, maybe the corporate headquarters for Target or one of those financial-adviser firms that did so well until 2008. But this was no office.

Well, it was in that there were printers and desks and things, but it was actually a branch of the FBI, the Bureau of False Flag Ops.

After I parked, I took the elevator to the correct floor, slid my key card through the slot, waited for the retinal scan, then popped in. Five minutes early! Victory was mine.

As always, I was greeted by Opus, the custodian for my floor.

"Hi . . . Cadence."

"Hi, big guy. Have a nice night?"

Opus gave the question careful thought before answering. "Yes." Opus didn't understand the concept of small talk—he had savant syndrome (never, never use the phrase "idiot savant"; soooo twentieth century!)—but he could do incredible things with numbers, even if he couldn't write out a grocery list. He was a shambling bear of a man—well over six feet tall, with shaggy brown hair, bushy eyebrows, mud-colored eyes, and thick forearms. His two-piece brown uniform made him look not unlike a grizzly bear. With a mop.

I'll admit, I had a soft spot for the man. I'd had to defend him from occasional taunts from some of my less sensitive co-workers, "rain man" being a popular insult.

It was almost funny that anybody who worked for BOFFO would have the nerve to insult anyone else who worked for BOFFO. After all, we all had—

"Cadence!" George Pinkman was actually dancing from one foot to the other. "I got the new *Halo*! You should come over and help me blow shit up."

"Some other time," I replied sweetly. George gave me the creeps. A textbook sociopath, he didn't think anything was real except the world of violent video games. Why BOFFO needed him I would never understand, but I was certainly in no position to complain or judge. I mean, jeepers! I was a federal cop, not King Solomon. "But thanks."

"Maybe your sister, then."

I shivered and moved past him to my desk. He really *was* crazy. Well, sure. He had a BOFFO ID card, didn't he? And he'd fooled a lot of people with those big green eyes, aquiline nose, and firm jaw. His eyebrows were slashing commas across his forehead, and although he had a slim build, he held no fewer than three black belts. He often dressed and talked effeminately to provoke the local rednecks. Then he'd lure them out into the parking lot and break various bones. All in the name of self-defense, of course, while sporting one of his huge collection of incredibly garish and tasteless neckties.

The one he wore now featured a single cartoon puppy in a dead-Christ pose, against a background of rainbows.

I scanned the morning faxes, checked arrest reports, did some work on the computer, and heated up my Hot Pocket, which I gobbled in six bites (*so* hungry!). I got a Frappuccino from the vending machine, balanced it on my Hello Kitty mouse pad, and began gulping it with a few Advils. This would, I hoped, take care of my hangover.

"Cadence Jones!"

I swung around in my chair, nearly spilling my drink. My supervisor, Michaela, was framed in the doorway of Da Pitt (where all her field agents congregated to fight crime and work on their Secret Santa drawings). She was a fifty-something woman with silver, straight chin-length hair and amazing green eyes. Pure green, not hazel. Like leaves! Hair the color of precious metal, eyes the color of wet leaves—she'd have been gorgeous if she hadn't been so scarily efficient and surrounded by cubicles and printers and mail carts. And today, as usual, she was dressed in Ann Taylor.

I squashed the urge to shake the ringing out of my ears—the boss lady had the volume and pitch of a steamer whistle. "Weren't we going to work on our inside voice?"

"Debriefing! Thirty minutes!"

"I know, I saw the e-mail." I pointed at my computer screen. "But thanks for assuming I hadn't learned to read in the first grade."

"Leave the mouth at your desk!" Thankfully, she vanished through another doorway.

Now how was I supposed to do that? Physically, it was impossible. Figuratively, it didn't make any sense, since my mouth was essentially what made me valuable to BOFFO. Maybe Michaela was coming off an odd night, too.

George shoved, hard, and his chair shot over to my desk. "It's Miller time!" he chortled, pounding his fists on his thighs.

It was a bad joke, of course. Connie Miller, who had poisoned four of her five children in seven years

(Why did she let the oldest live? What was it about the others? Why why why did she)

was being remanded for trial this morning; George and I were to baby-sit her until the local cops came. It was essentially some last-minute paperwork before transfer. Strictly custodial. Mornings like this reminded me that for fearless minions of the federal government, an awful lot of what we did was cleanup. For which we received full medical and dental, so it wasn't all bad.

Connie Miller creeped me out as much as George did, but for entirely different reasons. Call me old-fashioned, but it was against the laws of nature when moms killed their kids.

And Munchausen by proxy? Getting off on the attention you got when your kids got sick (by your own hand) and died? Weird. Repulsive. Horrifying. I was superglad my sister had helped make the collar; there was no way I could have taken her on my own.

It had become a matter for BOFFO when Miller moved from California to Minnesota. George and my sister had managed to track and nail her. Now the only thing left for BOFFO was routine paperwork, and putting the dead babies out of our minds. Two of the babies she had killed she'd conceived only after spending a great deal of time and money on fertility treatments.

Baffling.

We moved through various secure areas, slipping key cards through scanner after scanner. There were very few security guards at BOFFO: too many of us were paranoid and would begin acting like inmates. (Some of us, I suspected, had been in the past.) So whatever security could be automated, was.

Connie Miller was sitting quietly in an interrogation room, dressed in a lime jumpsuit with BOFFO printed in black letters on the back and sleeves. She was handcuffed in front, as she was deemed docile, cooperative, and even oddly friendly, not to mention in her early forties and overweight.

"Ms. Miller!" George called. "Ready for your day in court?"

"I can't wait," she replied, twinkling up at George. Her blue eyes (almost, I hated to admit, the exact same shade as mine) were wide and practically glowing. "The jury will believe me, once I explain everything."

"Don't forget to mention how you used peach puree to cover up the acidic taste of the poison," George suggested amiably. He yawned and scrubbed his face with his palms; he'd been up until the wee hours playing computer games, no doubt. "The jury will eat it up. Get it? Eat it up? Heh. You do realize your poor dead babies are going to be waiting for you in hell, right?"

I resisted the urge to kick him in the ankle. For one thing, George was an atheist. Rather, he did believe in God, and he believed *he* was that God. For another, he wouldn't have minded if Miller had killed twenty babies. George, like all sociopaths, lived for fun, passion, and challenges. Morality wasn't just an alien concept for him, it was utterly unknown.

No, he was just fucking with her. It was cruel, even for someone like her. Whatever we were, we were *professionals*.

I forced a smile, ignoring the throbbing in my temples. "If you could just sign here. And here. And initial here." It was a little like accepting a package from FedEx. "And sign here."

Connie obediently scribbled with the soft-felt-tip pen I'd handed her.

George sprawled himself in a chair opposite her and stroked his dead-rainbow-Jesus-dog tie. "Your problem is, you got greedy. One baby, okay. Two? Prob'ly would've worked. But four? And you crossed state lines? And let every hospital have your chart?"

"I can explain everything," she muttered, her red hair falling into her eyes as she huddled over the paperwork I was handing across the table.

"Tell it to the judge, sweetie." Like many sociopaths, George was charismatic and could make an insult sound like a flirtation. He was even leering at her, which would only confuse the poor woman.

It wasn't the first time I'd questioned Michaela's judgment in putting a pure sociopath on the team. They were just so darned unpredictable, not to mention unreliable when it came to pulling their weight at the Secret Santa party.

"You can't talk to me like that," the killer said primly. "The Lord has blessed me with many babies and many challenges."

"Challenges!" George hooted.

"Stop it," I pleaded. What was his point, other than to upset her? She had been caught. The jury would put her away. She'd spend the next thirty years in Shakopee. There was no point to this and it was upsetting the prisoner.

And *me.*

"Yes, *stop it*!" she shrieked, and lunged over the table at me. I stepped away from her and

Chapter Two

caught her by the wrist, twisted, ignored her howl, and flipped her away from me.

"Ohhhhhh!" someone chortled. "And Shiro sinks a three-pointer *right before the buzzer*!"

George Pinkman. Of course. "Be quiet," I snapped. Connie Miller came up for me, clawing, shrieking something about how my children were not safe from the whims of the Lord, how she was the Angel of Death, how she would separate the wheat from the yak-yak-yak. The prattling set my teeth on edge and made it easy to break her arm at the elbow, just so I could hear something different come out of those sweaty, nonsense-mongering lips.

Foolish woman. I could understand her initial mistake, as Cadence was an idiot who could not defend herself against a paper cut, but once I was there, what was the point of pissing me off?

Perhaps she was fooled by my size. Like many Asian Americans, I was a bit short.

It was hard to talk over Miller's screams, but I managed. "You have explaining to do, George Pinkman."

"What?" Being a bully, he was amazed when things went too far, and did not make the connection between his comments and her reaction. "She's the psycho, not me." He laughed, a nasty sound and entirely out of place amid the screams of pain.

A single guard raced into the room, trying to look everywhere at once. He secured Ms. Miller's hands—this time behind her back—and hauled her away, presumably to the infirmary. I did not especially care where they took her, so long as I did not have to listen to the wailing.

On his way out the door, he turned. "You all right, Cadence?"

"That's not Cadence," George the everlasting blabbermouth said. "That's Shiro."

As always, I was amazed to be confused with my sister. We looked, spoke, and acted nothing alike. Could this guard not see that? He was trained security, one of the few we had! Maybe we needed to go full automation. . . .

Maybe there was something in the nose. . . .

"Special Agent Jones, then," the guard corrected himself, unruffled.

"I am fine. She was unable to injure me." What a pity I could not say the same about George. Every time he opened his mouth he injured me. What a terrible man! But I knew perfectly well why Michaela partnered him with me. . . . I was the balance to his checks. It showcased her wisdom and bureaucratic ruthlessness.

George watched the guard take Miller away. "Yeah, you

know there's gonna be more paperwork, right? I don't mean a little more, a Post-it more, I mean reams."

I stifled a sigh. Sadly, he was right. Everlasting paperwork, the bane of law enforcement. A thirty-second incident would require three hours of documentation.

"I know."

"*You* can do it," he told me, as if I took orders from any man. "You're the one who broke her damn arm. They probably heard the snap all the way down Nicollet Avenue."

I eyed him and thought about breaking *his* arm. But more paperwork I did not need. Also, such an action would result in even more sessions with the idiotic Dr. Nessman.

I checked my watch. "We have a debriefing. The paperwork will wait."

With George trotting at my heels and my identity card flashing through all the right automated checkpoints, we made it to Da Pitt in less than five minutes. The other agents and Michaela were already seated. We took the last two empty chairs. Almost the entire Minneapolis staff was here—like most federal bureaucracies, we were a small field office that reported to a much larger office in D.C. Sometimes I shuddered to think about the lunatics that must be running around *that* building. They probably recruited straight from the Clinton and Bush administrations.

"Thanks for joining us, Cadence," my supervisor said in the only tone she knew—sarcastic.

"Wrong," I replied in the tone only I could get away with when speaking with Michaela.

Michaela blinked. "Oh. Sorry, Shiro. Didn't recognize you right away."

"Wait till you hear—aagghhh!" George lifted his foot up and cradled it like a baby. Like all sociopaths, he could handle anyone's pain but his own. Everyone else around the table looked startled, but no one dared to chastise me for the heel shot.

Like the rest of BOFFO, we ignored his shriek. A day without a sociopath's agony is a day without sunshine.

"Hey, hi, Shiro, no offense, but do you think Cadence could come back?" Tina McNamara said, indulging in her tic—she was snapping her fingers in a rapid, complicated tattoo. "I'm having a housewarming party on the fifth and I was hoping to invite her." *Snap-snap, snappity snap-snap-snap.* "It's always so much more of a good time if she comes. Everyone just loves her to death."

"A . . . party?" I managed not to choke on the word.

"Maybe you could leave her a note. Oh, and tell her to bring a side dish. Maybe that pasta salad she learned off Rachael Ray?"

I loathed Rachael Ray.

"With the chicken and the tomatoes?"

Almost as much as I loathed tomatoes. I eyed Tina with real distaste and

Chapter Three

found myself in the briefing room. Which was mega-weird, since the last thing I remembered was Connie Miller lunging at me. I sneaked a peek at my watch. Nine minutes, gone. Long gone. And George, for some strange reason, was holding his foot and groaning.

"What?" I asked, assuming someone had been talking to me.

"Oh, good, you're back," cute little Tina McNamara said. She was a teeny brunette with brown eyes and quick hands. Unbeatable on the firing range (except for my sister) and (so it was said) in the bedroom (except for my other sister), she threw a wonderful party. "Can you come to my housewarming on the fifth?"

"Really?" Ooooh, I love parties! "I'd *love* to! Can I bring anything?"

"Rachael fucking Ray's fucking pasta salad," George hissed, massaging the top of his foot.

"Jeepers, are you okay?"

"Shut the fuck up."

"If everyone is finished," Michaela said calmly, "perhaps we can get some work done?"

And so the debriefing on the ThreeFer Killer began.

Chapter Four

I love crime scenes.

I guess that sounds pretty bad, and I apologize. But to be perfectly honest, there's nothing like it. It's not just the puzzle it represents (who? why? and why today? why not yesterday, or tomorrow? and will he/she do it again? and if so, why why *why*?), it's the camaraderie—the team pulling together.

It's drinking bad coffee out of dirty cups. It's teasing Wenkum because his wife kicked him out again, and teasing Nadia because she's getting pretty heavy in her second trimester. It's avoiding Beth if it's a rape scene because she has a—a—she has a thing. A bad thing.

It's—you know. Well, maybe you do know, being a criminal psychiatrist and all. For me, a crime scene is wonderful because I know I belong there. Even better, everyone else on scene knows I belong there. There! Now how many people can say that about their job? And who wants to attach herself to an office cube? Or run tar alongside a new street?

And don't get me started on the adrenaline rush. And—

this is going to sound awful—I feel proud that I can flash my ID and get waved past yellow crime-scene tape, get as close as I want to the bodies. It's gross, but cool. None of the reporters or public can get that close—not without cheating—but I can.

In addition to a brand-new puzzle to solve (and oh Lord, I *love* puzzles), there is the delicate balancing act between the Feebs and the local police.

And it's not the Feebs' fault! So you mustn't blame them. The average street cop will draw his gun a couple dozen times in the course of a career. An FBI agent? Maybe three times in a career. *Maybe.* And our agents . . . well, of course, we don't even have guns. (Some say this is for the sake of public safety, but my sister believes it's a matter of cost efficiency. After all, *she's* never needed one.) Anyway, most federal agents specialize in investigation, computer manipulation, voice recognition, that sort of thing. So if you meet a Feeb who's in his or her late forties, you think to yourself, Wow, he's got tons of experience!

But in city-cop years, that forty-something Feeb is maybe . . . five? Yeah. That sounds about right. A kindergarten fed.

The cops' disdain doesn't stretch to BOFFO, because most of the people on the planet don't know about BOFFO. We see quite a bit of action, but it's not like we can ever talk to a reporter about it or anything. Hello, reporter, good-bye, funding.

Besides, it doesn't matter who draws and who doesn't. Who sets up a computer sting and who chases the bad guy while sirens wail and

(geese)

children scatter.

I just want to catch the guy. I don't care how it gets done, and I don't care who gets the credit—credit for our bureau would be a *disaster* for us. And I think that's probably the only reason the Minneapolis cops actually help us. Especially me.

Not to brag or anything, but I'm pretty good at talking to them. They like talking to me, they like taking credit, they like the fade we do as they solve the case. And that helps us all play nice.

"My, my," Detective Clapp said, slurping at—judging from his jittery countenance—his fifth or sixth cup of coffee that morning. "Look what the dog barfed up."

"You be nice," I said reproachfully. I had pulled the powder blue paper booties over my sneakers (Michaela could be a slave driver, but she didn't care how we dressed . . . in fact, since most people didn't know about BOFFO, she *didn't* want us looking too much like federal agents) and now crossed to him, carefully skirting the photographers and the CSI agents, and hoping no one would spill coffee on my butter yellow T-shirt and faded jeans. I flinched back as an investigator darted past me and took a quick succession of pictures and—whew! Didn't trip.

Oh, and while I'm on the subject: I would never, ever imply that the CSI folks aren't helpful, because they are, and we couldn't do our job without them. But they don't solve crimes like it's shown on TV. None of what we do is anything like TV. They collect evidence and write reports and give the reports to us. *We* solve crimes.

Did that sound conceited? I didn't mean it to. I guess I just wanted to set things straight. Does that mean I'm vain, or just anxious for people to know the truth? Might have to mention that in my next session . . . unless you don't want to talk about it. It's okay if you don't want to talk about it.

"D'you want a cup?" Clapp was saying, offering me a plastic cup full of vile-smelling sludge.

"Thanks," I said, because I didn't want to hurt his feelings. I'd almost rather drink my own vomit than choke down a cup of—

I'm sorry. That was disgusting. Can we scratch that? Put it down to a stressful morning. . . . It's not every day I wake up to purple vibrators and lemon slices in my bathroom.

"I hate to wreck your morning, blondie, but it looks like we've got another one from the ThreeFer."

I stared down at the crime scene, hoping none of the reporters (how did they get there so *fast*?) were getting a zoom shot of my inordinately large ass. It was definitely textbook ThreeFer, a nickname George had come up with that, as these things sometimes do, had stuck.

The ThreeFer Killer always took victims in threes (thus the catchy nickname). He always left exactly three bodies. This time he'd left his awful mess on the corner of Chicago and Lake, which meant we needed to clear the scene ASAP or some poor little kid in the area would have nightmares for the rest of the year.

Ah. The other thing. The crime scenes were always outside and in fairly open spaces. We had yet to find a ThreeFer victim who had been dead longer than ten hours. And that in itself was a puzzle, if you thought about it. Certainly it made things more risky for the killer. So why do it?

Well. Why do crazy people do anything?

And who would know better than a BOFFO agent?

They do it out of compulsion.

They do it because they can't see any other way to do things.

They do it because the voices in their heads won't let them rest unless they do it *that very specific way*. Every single time.

Poor bum. ThreeFer was doing awful things, but it seemed to me he had been a victim *first*. And now a slave to the rituals he forced himself to complete. I could feel sorry for him, but that wouldn't stop me from catching him.

"Shit on toast," George said, yawning. He was on his second cup of coffee already—black. Yech! Why not just suck on the coffee grounds, get the caffeine jolt that way? "Probably should have paid more attention in the briefing."

"Yes." I could have said a few more things but didn't. But yes—we had just had an extensive briefing on this killer, one George had practically slept through.

"What was the gist?"

"Check your notebook," I advised sweetly, knowing full well my charmingly sociopathic partner hadn't written down a thing that morning—except maybe the phone number of the new redheaded temp in Processing.

I had *my* notebook out, and, looking smugly officious, I scribbled in it. Among other things, there was a perfectly nice hotel not three blocks from here—had the killer stayed there? This wasn't the only state he'd dumped vics; he could be from anywhere in the Midwest—maybe even anywhere in the country. The hotel was a place to start—and probably not much else. Time to talk to the manager, the housekeepers, the chambermaids, the loading-dock fellas.

"Aw, come on, Cadence," George whined. "Give me a break.

I was, like, all freaked out when your sister committed felony assault earlier."

"Sure you were." As if George "Psychoboy" Pinkman were freaked out by anything that didn't directly affect his id or ego.

"*Caaaaaa*-dence . . ."

I hated when he said my name through a nasal whine. But I kept jotting (at least *one* of us could be a professional, for gosh sakes!), noting the local businesses within thirty yards of the bodies. More people to question. Security-camera film to subpoena and stare at for hours. Cops knocking door to door to door. That's where the locals were invaluable. They'd do the door-to-door interviews, write the reports, scarf up all the scut work, the legwork. They'd pick through hundreds of pounds of garbage, search hundreds of yards of carpet, sidewalk, and street for the tiniest hair, the smallest bit of trace evidence. If anything looked promising, they'd send one of BOFFO to reinterview.

Yeah, it's part of that process where civilians get peeved because they have to tell the same story four times to eight people. And who could blame them?

It's ironic I'm in this business, because sometimes crime solving isn't as much like puzzle solving as it is like capture the flag.

"Never one victim," I told George, taking pity on him. Which was a large error in judgment, as he had never, and would never, take pity on me. "Always three."

"Aha!" George crowed. "Thus ThreeFer. I get it now. Oh. Wait. I already knew that."

I tried to wither him with a look, but George had been

glared at by the best—including both my sisters. Everything rolled off him like water off a duck. Or blood off a mirror.

"Always left out in the open, so they're found quickly. It's in our lap because he's crossed state lines."

He snorted. "Jeez, thanks. *That* I knew."

Nice try, George! But you wanted the gist, and now you're getting it. I tried to make my voice as drony and snore-inducing as possible. "One set of victims in Minot, North Dakota. Another set in Des Moines. You remember Des Moines."

George pinched the bridge of his nose and sighed. "Unfortunately. Everything I packed came back smelling like pig shit. I fucking hate Iowa. It's not a state. It's an asylum staffed with pig farmers."

"Well, you would know more about that than I," I answered, grinning. "So things *are* coming back to you; how wonderful. You'll also recall—I hope—that you and I had to check out the Des Moines crime scene, spent hours with the locals, interviewed all sorts of—"

"Idiots, and for nothing. Des Moines was a dead end. Des Moines was disco and dodo birds."

He was right, so I moved on. "One more set of three vics in Pierre."

"Which smelled worse than Des Moines."

"At least your priorities never change. And now he's in Minneapolis. You and I—"

"Are going to kill each other one day." He sighed.

"—are on point," I finished.

"You mean you, and I, and Shiro, and—"

"Don't say the name!" I nearly shrieked. The *last* thing we needed right now was for *her* to show up.

"What is she, Voldemort? Christ." George pretended to wipe his cheek. "All right, calm down, say it, don't spray it."

"Cadence!" George and I turned to look; Officer Lynn Rivers was hurrying toward us. She was a stereotypical corn-fed blonde (that hair! those gorgeous blue eyes! and those *legs*!); I'm sure I wasn't the only one who noticed how very nicely she filled out her uniform. Her short hair ruffled in the breeze, obscuring her eyes, and for a minute she looked like a Viking maiden heading to a fjord. A maiden with a gun. Did you head to a fjord or, you know, make one?

George in particular was trying not to slobber into his coffee cup. "I was hoping you'd catch the squeal," Lynn was saying. "This look like your bad guy from Pierre?"

"I'm afraid so. Also Des Moines."

"Enough about fucking Des Moines," George whined. "Iowa! The dullest state in the Union! The state flower is a rose. A *pink* rose."

Lynn looked a bit taken aback, but I was used to the rant. I could even tell her what was coming.

"State bird," I whispered to her.

"And the state bird is a canary! Which eats dandelion seeds and ragweed. And the state plant is the oak tree. An oak tree! Did they try to bore me out of my tits by picking boring-ass shit as their emblems?"

"Yes," I agreed, "because it's all about you, George."

"Well"—he shrugged—"it usually is."

Sadly, George was utterly serious. Poor Lynn had been here ten seconds and looked like she wished she were still stuck in traffic.

We shook hands; hers were small, and I often wondered

how she managed to pull the trigger on her Beretta M9. I was *very* relieved she'd given up the .38 after that nasty business with an otherwise perfectly harmless dentist who liked to jam his lady friends' left arms into his garbage disposals.

Lynn had uselessly plinked away at him with the .38 until she'd run out of ammo, and then my younger sister—well, I didn't remember, and Lynn had been unconscious by then, but there were pieces of Dr. Demento strewn from his office all the way to the parking lot. True to BOFFO regs, the whole thing was hushed up, Lynn was given all the credit, and the name Cadence (or any other) Jones was never mentioned.

"I'm glad to see you, Lynn. We'll need all the help we can get."

"No doubt." She turned to the side and tapped her hip because, silly girl, she assumed I hadn't immediately noticed the new gun. Don't get me wrong; .38s were fine weapons . . . if you wanted to play pin the tail on the donkey. "Does this gun make me look fat?"

"Oh, stop it." I took another sip and shuddered. Lynn kindly took the cup from me to "share" and then "accidentally" dropped it.

Because she was an excellent cop (and with only six years of street experience!), she had anticipated me. Because she was nice (father a minister, mother a nurse), we were friends, sort of—maybe friendly was a better way to put it. She knew my secret, anyway.

But she was the only one who liked Adrienne better than Shiro or me. I tried not to take it personally. After all, Adrienne had saved her life.

Still, it stung. I tried to and generally resisted the impulse to suggest she see a psychiatrist. (That's the thing about people in therapy. We all think everyone should be in therapy. And everyone should! The fact that we're right just makes things trickier.)

And Lynn was a rare creature—she thought an entire department of armed, crazy federal agents was a fine plan. Congress, by contrast, didn't always get on board. Most people didn't, in fact. It was almost like they felt the disadvantages of putting schizophrenic kleptomaniac sociopathic multiple personality depressives in the field outweighed the benefits. Which only proves that many people have no imagination.

Okay, I think I'm done being silly now. Sure, on the face of it BOFFO looks like the FBI lost a bet. Heck, my own best friend has suggested on more than one occasion that any advantages Adrienne gives me are far outweighed by all the felony assaults she's added to my jacket.

What my friend doesn't understand, being an unemployed artist, that Lynn, a cop, does, is that I am an effective federal agent *because of* my psychological quirks. (Quirks may not be the strongest word, to be fair.) Lynn understands that a sociopath like George thinks nothing of bending a few rules to get his man. She gets that a kleptomaniac knows how to take things away from a bad guy right under his nose. She knows that a histrionic can turn in an Oscar-worthy performance in any undercover situation.

Helpful? Sure. A pain in the butthole? Yes. Worth the hassle to get the job done? Well. We have an eight-figure budget that sails through congressional budget justification every single year. What does that tell you?

"We're already canvassing the neighborhood," Lynn was telling me, foolishly assuming I had been paying attention, "knocking on every door. We're focusing on the businesses that were open last night; there were quite a few. So far nobody's seen anything."

"Of course not."

"This asshole's got the luck of the devil," George commented. And he wasn't far wrong. Multiple crime scenes, multiple vics, for the last year . . . and we were no closer to getting him or her now than we had been when George and I drove to the airport for our fun-filled Iowa field trip.

"We'll keep at it. But you should come over here. There's something my boss wants you to see."

Oh, goody. Nothing like staring down at a triple homicide to make a Hot Pocket surge back up a greasy esophagus. Blurgh.

I followed Lynn, carefully skirting photographers and what we called "the props," those little yellow plastic numbers you placed beside various pieces of evidence, both to get a system in place and to have an idea of the size of the item. No matter how bloody and awful the crime scene, no matter how many times you had nightmares about it, no matter if you'd memorized the file, you'd be surprised what you get wrong on the witness stand weeks or months or years later.

When you're testifying in court, it helps to look at a picture and realize the item in question couldn't be more than six inches high or four inches wide. Like that.

And it doesn't matter if you are a local sheriff, a beat cop, a Feeb, a deputy, or a member of the Secret Service. Crime scenes are all processed in essentially the same way.

Interview. Examine. Photograph. Sketch. Process. And around and around we go.

In addition to the adrenaline rush and the knowledge that there is a new puzzle to solve, crime scenes are fun for me because I get to meet new people—and not just the dead ones. Heck, other than my sisters and George, Lynn and Clapp were practically friends. (Actually, adding George to that list was an act of charity. . . . I wasn't sure a pure sociopath *could* have friends.)

Case in point: Jim Clapp was dragging another man toward our small group, someone I didn't know.

"What's this?" the new guy was saying. "An actual *pleasant* surprise at one of these bloodbaths? I knew it was going to be a great day when I found *two* secret decoder rings in my Lucky Charms."

I blushed and stuffed my hands in my pockets. "Three stab wounds," I said, almost wishing I had another cup of the awful coffee. "Hardly a bath of any sort."

The new guy—a detective, judging from the okay suit and gold shield—was about my height, with prematurely white hair (because there wasn't a wrinkle to be found on that face unless you counted the laugh lines) and a swimmer's build, all narrow, sinewy strength and wide shoulders.

"You must be the famous Special Agent Jones," he continued. "Lynn's told me quite a bit about you, but nobody said you were such a cutie."

"That's not true," Clapp said. "I told you that ten minutes ago."

"Right before *I* told you comments on women's physical attributes have no place at a crime scene," Lynn said primly.

"Aw, it's our fault you're so cute?" George cried. He reached out (the sociopath's disregard for personal space) and tried to pinch her cheek. "Cute, cute, key-yute!"

She backed away with a look that suggested she wanted to try out her new gun.

"Go give someone a parking ticket, buddy," the detective ordered absently, smacking George's palm away from Lynn's face with one hand and extending me the other. I clasped it and reveled in his smoky voice. "I'm Detective Ben Papp."

Papp? As in smear? Oh, the poor man.

"Nice to meet you, though I'm sorry these are the circumstances."

I extricated my hand with some difficulty; Papp had a grip like rubber cement. "Hazard of the trade."

"Worse than being an Avon lady," George piped up.

Papp ignored him, which I found enchanting. "Your boss told my boss you get first walk, and when the Feebs command, we locals tremble and obey." He smiled, so I was pretty sure he was teasing. "We didn't do it that way in Spokane, but who in his right mind would come to Spokane anyway? *Is* there even an FBI branch near Spokane?"

"There's one in Seattle," George said helpfully. The breeze kicked up and whipped his tie across his face. He chewed on it absently for a moment, then spit it out.

"Okay," I said, hoping I didn't sound as mystified as I felt. "Well, come on over. We've got most of the documentation, but I imagine you'll want some of your own guys to get in here."

"Cadence needs to walk it before any of the other Feebs," Clapp reminded him.

"We know," half the cops on the scene said in unison. Cops

were good at looking like they were focusing on something else while they were actually sucking in every bit of info they could. Meaning: they had heard every word of our "private" conversation and were anxious for the Feebs to get on with it. And who could blame them?

All Papp did was laugh. Thank goodness. How to explain that everything I looked at would be studied, analyzed, and obsessed over by three people? All living in the same body? What I would miss, Shiro would catch. What she caught and dismissed, our other sister would chase down and choke the truth out of. What they both thought irrelevant, I could fit into the rest of the puzzle.

I'm sorry about its all being so complicated.

Chapter Five

Two men, one woman. The triple-victim pattern was like that in Minot, in Des Moines, in Pierre, and now here. All stabbed with what the coroner thought was a good-sized fillet knife—something to do the job quickly, something easy to keep sharp. Something not out of place in the average kitchen. (You want to lose all interest in cooking? Visit a kitchen-based crime scene. I promise you'll have to do it only once.) No other bruises on the bodies; they weren't beaten or dragged. They just showed up dead.

Profiling the victims had been an exercise in mind-numbing futility. They were all different ages and races. ThreeFer had killed busboys and physicians; men and women; an alcoholic and a marathon runner, for heaven's sake. Tox screens always came back negative, except for booze—and not every time, either. Some of the victims had been seriously impaired, some stone-cold sober. BACs came back anywhere from 0.0 to 0.11.

Because we had been unable to find commonality in the victims, we were nowhere on our profile. Until we figured out the connections the victims had to ThreeFer, we had more crime scenes to look forward to—a distressing thought, to put it mildly.

Shoot, we didn't even know when the victims had been taken. Time of death could be deduced, but some of the victims had spent half a day or more with their killer—and some of them hadn't even been reported missing before the body showed up. About the only thing we'd been able to figure was that ThreeFer was taking each victim one at a time, then dumping three bodies sometime later.

The bodies were always dumped somewhere semipublic (lab advised they were all killed elsewhere, and dumped where a civilian would find them and call a cop—and never in a neighborhood where a civilian would find them and not bother), and these were no exception; they were in an alley, easily visible from the sidewalk. Yes, about the only thing we could be completely sure of was that the victims had been killed elsewhere, then discarded with another awful verse.

The verses! Another puzzle, another frustrating clue that no one could figure. ThreeFer left an excerpt from a Shakespearean sonnet at each crime scene.

Pierre:

Like as the waves make towards the pebbled shore,/So do our minutes hasten to their end;/Each changing place with that which goes before/In sequent toil all forwards do contend.

Des Moines:

Music to hear, why hear'st thou music sadly?/Sweets with sweets war not, joy delights in joy:/Why lov'st thou that which thou receiv'st not gladly,/Or else receiv'st with pleasure thine annoy?

Minot:

For thou art so possessed with murd'rous hate/That 'gainst thy self thou stick'st not to conspire,/Seeking that beauteous roof to ruinate/Which to repair should be thy chief desire.

And here, in Minneapolis, courtesy of Officer Rivers's iPod:

Not from the stars do I my judgment pluck,/And yet methinks I have astronomy;/But not to tell of good or evil luck,/Of plagues, of dearths, or season's quality.

"Oh, fuck me till I cry." George sighed. He disliked Shakespeare. Me, I could take or leave the Bard; I just wanted to figure out what the sonnets had to do with anything. So far nobody had a clue.

In keeping with our mysterious fair-haired serial killer, all the sonnets had been printed somewhere on ordinary copy paper with a run-of-the-mill printer—zillions of possibilities in Minnesota alone.

"Maybe a college professor?" Lynn was asking, rereading the sonnet on her screen. "Or a—I dunno, a poet? An artist?"

"A dumbass psycho nutbag?" George asked, raking his fingers through his hair. "Welcome to the info age, baby. You don't have to have any time in college to pump out Shakespearean sonnets. All you have to do is Google."

Annoyingly, that was a good point.

But this time, *this* time, there was something new. Thank goodness, finally, hallelujah, something new. The female, vic one (I'm sorry to sound so cold, but I had to call them something until they got ID'd), had the front page of the *Star Tribune* pinned to her chest . . . from January 1, 2003.

Vic two, the shorter of the men, also had paper pinned to his shirt—a desk calendar from December 15, 2003. And vic three, the tall, fat one, had a poster of—of—

"Is that what I think it is?" George asked, covering his mouth so the other cops wouldn't see him smirk. But heavens knew I was used to it.

"It's a poster of the Three Tenors."

"Stapled to his forehead!"

"The big jerk," I muttered.

"Ah, come on, Cadence, what's your beef against big boy singers?" George squatted by the body and peered closely at the poster. "Y'know, you ought to let yourself go once in a while. 'Big jerk'? Call him an asshole. Call him a sick fuck. Call him a twisted—"

"Why now?" I mused. I was as close to the body as I could safely get without messing up evidence. Same again: stab wound to the chest. No defensive wounds. How was he stabbing them without their fighting back?

"Weird," a new voice said, and I looked up. Then straightened in a hurry. "They don't ever fight him. Weird."

"Jerry," I began warningly.

"Weird weird weird."

"You better behave."

"Oh shit on a brick!" my partner exploded. "Who let *you* past the tape?"

Our colleague, Jerry Nance, blinked big wet hurt eyes at us. He was dressed like a typical fed, in what looked like an off-the-rack suit, black socks, loafers, and a boring solid blue tie. Only George and I knew he had meticulously made the suit by hand, and it had taken months. The suit concealed dozens of hidden pockets.

He was slender, tall, and balding. His high forehead was sunburned and peeling; his pale blue eyes were watery and vague. He looked, moved, and spoke like an amiable midwesterner. He was, in fact, from Italy, spoke nine languages, and had three college degrees and an IQ of 162.

He had the soul of a clerk, and lived for making lists, examining evidence, putting things in their place, and relentlessly alphabetizing everything he could get his hands on.

He was brilliant and invaluable at crime scenes.

He was also a kleptomaniac.

"How long have you been here?" I asked, dreading the answer.

He blinked. "Just got here."

"Then what's . . . *this*?" I groped for his suit pocket and withdrew . . . the wrapper to a pack of Sno Balls.

"Jerry, oh good sweet Christ!" George looked like he was going to make Jerry eat the Sno Ball wrapper, and I moved so I was between them.

"Where'd you get it, Jer?"

"The trash can by the door."

"You got that from the scene?" Lynn asked, horrified. "You—you took that out of the trash can at a scene we're still processing? But—"

"Bad Jerry!" George was yelling, trying to reach around me to punch Jerry's balding head. "Bad bad bad! We've been over this! And over it! You idiotic pervy nerdy sticky-fingered asshole!"

"It's not the killer's," Jerry explained. "A customer from the bar left it." I had no idea how Jerry knew that; I only knew he was correct. He was always right about stuff like that. As I said, invaluable on scene. Also aggravating—he couldn't *not* lift something.

George and I knew how important Jerry Nance was to BOFFO by the complete lack of trouble he got in when he interfered with crime scenes. But the locals were staring, so I got moving.

"Thank you, Agent Nance," I said with exquisite charm and politeness. "I—I hadn't realized your point until you, um, acted it out by showing us how the killer, um, didn't eat Sno Balls at the scene."

Jerry blinked at me again. "He didn't eat anything. But he read the crossword and did the whole thing in—"

"Fas-ih-fuckin'-ating," George said. "Get lost, Nance. Go count staplers in the office supply store across the street."

Jerry brightened and hurried away. I struggled to get back to my train of thought. Ah! The poster. "Why change the MO so quickly?"

"Because he thinks we're stupid."

"And why is he—or she—escalating?"

"What are you, new in school? Why do they all escalate? They get off on being God. Who could give that up? Believe me, I know of what I speak," George added, but I didn't rise to the bait. I had zero interest in how George had ended up in BOFFO. Shiro knew but wouldn't tell me. It was probably just as well.

Besides, he was right. Our killer was escalating and sowing more clues because he was frustrated—we, the stupid cops and Feebs, weren't getting it. So he had to show us. And show us. And show us.

And he was escalating because he thought we were stupid, unworthy of his genius, and besides—he was God in his universe. We were only the audience.

I sighed and stood. "George, get on the horn with Michaela and make sure the other victims in the Dakotas didn't have any paperwork on them."

"But you know damned well they—"

"Just call, okay?" I puffed hair out of my eyes and made a conscious effort to lower my voice. "Will you just please follow procedure without being asked three times? Or five? Or agreeing you'll do it if I show you my breasts?"

"*Will* you show me your breasts?"

"George . . ."

"Okay, okay, just don't bring Shiro here, for Christ's sake." He was holding his hands up and backing away from me. "I'm doing it, okay? I don't think I've said okay this much in my entire life, okay, but I'm doing it, okay? So just calm down, okay?"

As if Shiro would ever get her hands dirty pounding

George's face into new and interesting shapes. Ah well. A girl could dream.

"This probably isn't the time or place," Clapp said cheerfully, "but are we still on for tonight?"

Ah! Tonight. Yes, after running into each other at dozens of crime scenes, Clapp had finally asked me out. I'd said yes, which was proof that I was crazy. See, Jim Clapp didn't know about my sisters. He just thought I was part of some elite FBI bad-guy unit. Also he was cute and single. And so was I. Well, single, anyway. Sort of.

Clapp had wild red hair which stuck up in all directions, no matter how much gel he lathered on it. He was famous for his gel. . . . He kept three tubes in his cruiser and God only knew how many in his locker. He had the pale face of the natural redhead, and gobs of freckles. He looked like Opie. Opie who could bench 270. He had to have his suits custom made, which was awful on his salary.

"Yeah." George leered. "Are ya?"

With an effort, I ignored my partner. "Yes, of course. Why don't I pick you up at the Cop Shop? Who wants to fight rush hour just to drive to Burnsville?" I was a sucker for gobs of pasta and mojitos, so I had established two days ago it was Buca Di Beppo or nothing.

"Cop Shop it is . . . seven o'clock okay?"

"Sure," I replied, hoping one of my sisters wouldn't arrive by then. I was nuts, agreeing to dinner with someone who had no idea I was clinically insane.

I was lonesome, too. So. There was that to consider.

Lynn was saying something, but I was being rude and not

listening. I had turned to look at the crime scene again. There was something about it. Well, there's something about *every* scene. Even at the most banal, even at a scene I'd

(we'd)

seen a dozen times before, something always reached out and plucked at

(us)

me.

Even in domestics, the most commonplace violent crime, something plucked. Wife beater crossed state lines and killed her in Minnesota? There wasn't a cop who'd been on the force two years who hadn't seen dozens of domestics. But why that night, why that woman, why that city? Why did they move? Why did the stress of unpacking not set him off, but the stress of her being late with McDonald's did?

Like I said before: Why now? Why these guys? Why this spot? Why again?

But this. The ThreeFer Killer. This was something else. And I didn't know what it was. It was like a tickle in my brain that wouldn't leave me alone. Tickle, heck—it was a *fishhook* in my brain that wouldn't leave me alone, digging and churning and scraping and—

I'm sorry. That was a disgusting image, wasn't it?

Could it be—was there something almost . . . *familiar* about this setup? The scenes in Pierre, Des Moines, and Minot? Familiar beyond the obvious?

Mysteries, mysteries.

Or perhaps not. Perhaps there wasn't a mystery here at all

(oh, but that's impossible)

it's possible that you already know everything you need to solve the crime

(it's not true it's not it's)

Go to sleep, Cadence.

"We've . . .

". . . we have seen

Chapter Six

this before."

Clapp's head tilted; I doubted he'd heard my dry voice before. George had, though, and was sidling close to me, a pained expression on his face.

"What the fuck are *you* doing here, Shiro, you horrible horrible thing?" George was smiling at me. Well. Showing his teeth. Odious man.

"As I said, we have seen this before. There is something here."

"Duh, there's something here. The Three goddamned Tenors are here, another stupid sonnet is here, not to mention a hundred cops who have no idea how completely fucked-up crazy you are. Will you please pretty please let Cadence come back now?"

It was amusing that Cadence had no idea why she had been partnered with George, why he never went off on her, why he respected her (as much as he could) and not anyone else at

BOFFO. I knew but would not tell. George was afraid of me. He was right to be afraid of me.

"Pretty please?" He was still babbling.

I gave him a long stare, and, since "sociopath" wasn't a synonym for "stupid," he actually backed off a step and dropped his gaze. Really, Cadence was too easy on this thug.

"I cannot let her back right now; she is no use when in denial." *Cadence, Cadence. What a child you are.*

I ducked under more crime tapes to take a closer look.

The Three Tenors.

January 1, 2003.

December 15, 2003.

Three victims—again. Stabbed through the heart—again. Left with calendars and posters—something new.

Something new in Minnesota.

Something new where I lived with my sisters. Where the *three of us* lived.

I walked past Clapp and said, "Our date is off." If I were nicer, the stricken look on his face might have moved me. But I am not. And so it did not.

"Wha—Wait. Cadence? You look funny. Are you feeling all right?"

He was not talking to *me*, so I ignored him. I turned in time to see Agent Nance on his knees, carefully going over the ground in front of the trash with the methodical, tireless precision he brought to everything. A man I could appreciate, though the compulsive stealing was puzzling. Ah well. A problem for another day.

I passed Cadence's local officer friend and said, "She warned you no fewer than six times."

Lynn, standing in approved cop mode (arms on hips, eyes narrow and squinty), did a double take. A silly, clichéd double take, like this was a comedy instead of real life. "What?"

"Six times, Officer Rivers. Your warnings. Six. And she should not have had to, even once. Thirty-eights are awful in the field. Just awful. It has been documented. Many times."

"Cadence, are you feeling all right?"

I managed not to roll my eyes. "You deserved worse." I paused, considering. "Though I am glad you lived. It would have been annoying and not at all cost-effective to pay your family death benefits and hire and train a new recruit."

Then—ugh! She was touching me. *They* were touching me. "I think it's the heat," Clapp said, looming on my left.

"You look pale. Are you gonna throw up, honey?" The female officer menacingly clutched my right hand.

"I am *not* going to throw up. *I*—"

"I wouldn't do that," George warned them, smiling.

"—have *never* thrown up. Now take your hands off me at—at—"

Geese.

"I have a point to make. We have seen this before. Stop touching me at once. My point—I have a point and you will *listen*!"

Geese.

Clapp's slimy grip, tightening. *Too close.* Rivers's wide face, leering. *Coffee breath.* George was the only one carefully backing off, which for some reason made me feel

geese

more out of control.

There were three geese flying overhead. Were they Canada geese? Oh God, were they? I could not I did not I would not would not would not I I I I I iiiiiiiiiiiiii

Chapter Seven

this before."

"This before."

"This before."

The man-boy Clapp now tilts his head,
tilts his head, tilts his head . . .
He does not know that I am here, I am here . . .
. . . allll daaaay looong, 'cause
The wheels on the bus go round and round . . .
. . . I am here . . .
. . . round and round . . .
George the Crotch gets closer now, closer now,
closer now, and the wheels on the bus . . .
"What the fuck

are you doing

here?"

He hisses.

I hiss back

"Hush,

There's something here,"

Something here,
Something here,
"Of course there is,"

he grumbles back.

"Three goddamned fucking Tenors are here, and
a hundred fucking cops with no idea how completely
fucked up you are yes I said it you're fucked up
and if you don't let Cadence back I'm going to stop
whispering and say it louder and cute Jimmy Clapp
will cancel your date and they'll put you in a
padded room where you belong and I'm not afraid of
you fucking bitch I don't care what you think and
don't look at me like that you know I hate that look
I'm just trying to solve this case like you we've
got a job to do so can you get Cadence back here
so we can fucking do it?"
Allllllllllll

Daaaaaaaaaaay

Loooooooooong

Wait.

We did that part already. He talked to Shiro. He doesn't know it's me

Know it's me
Know it's me
Surprise!
George the Crotch won't look me in the eye
Look me in the eye
Look me in the geese
And the wheels on the bus go

"Cadence can't come back,
she's not ready."
So I step up to a body and
See three tenors.
See how they sing.
Calendars and posters, calendars and posters,
Calendars and posters, calendars and posters,
Something borrowed, something new,
Something new, something new.
"It all looks cutie, but
Cadence?"
It's man-boy Clapp, who doesn't know,
Doesn't know,
Doesn't know.
"Date's off," I say,
and walk away.
Alllll daaaaay loooooong.
Heeeey . . . hellooooo, sis!

Chapter Eight

FROM THE PATIENT FILES OF DR. CHRISTOPHER NESSMAN
CASE FILE #216B
SUBJECT: SHIRO JONES

Shiro Jones, hereafter 216B (see Case files 216A and 216C, as well as Root file Jones-216, code-named HYDRA, EYES ONLY; written and verbal authorization from MOTHER required before access allowed), suffers from multiple personality disorder.

Though arguably the personality with the most serenity and emotional strength, 216B is also the most volatile.

216A is the group's most socially integrated member of the trio. She has friends, understands basic social mores, and conducts effective if limited engagement with local law personnel and other key partners.

216B is the group's secure hiding place . . . and usually (but not always) the first to emerge from 216A. She keeps 216A safe, emotionally and physically. She plays an enforcement role at times, both internally and externally.

216B's relationship to 216C is more difficult to characterize. If my suspicion is true—the "C" personality was created at the moment of defining trauma which caused dissociation—then "B" may have emerged later, as a "buffer" between the two dramatically different personalities. This would correspond with their perceived ages (B is the youngest at 23, C believes herself to be 24, and only A is correct in believing herself to be 27).

The personalities are as different physiologically as they are emotionally. Valium dosages appropriate for 216B generally risk overdose when administered to 216A and are not nearly enough to sedate 216C.

While hypnotism has had some enlightening and calming effects with 216B and her "sisters," I have noticed increasing resistance to hypnotic sessions. This is troubling, as switching personalities is quite a bit like a hypnotic suggestion in the first place; it is for that reason multiples exist. More disquieting, their resistance is a major roadblock to reintegration.

If they succeed in throwing off their interest and willingness to be put under, we will need to find some other way to (a) communicate with all three, (b) keep the two less socially adept personalities under control, and (c) find out another method to encourage integration. 216B was the first to develop resistant behavior—perhaps, again, a protective or mediating tactic, meant to keep the other two personalities separate.

Many of these findings have greater detail elsewhere in this file, but their examination is useful in reviewing the transcript of June 26 (attached).

TRANSCRIPT: AGENT INCIDENT REVIEW

01:20, SEPT 26, 2010

BOFFO REGIONAL OFFICE, MINNEAPOLIS

PSYCHIATRIST: NESSMAN

COMMENTS: Expectations were for agent 216A to arrive. Instead, 216B was dominant at the time. This is irregular behavior, as 216A is generally fastidious about keeping appointments.

Session begins 3120 hours, BOFFO building, Minneapolis, Minnesota

DR. NESSMAN: I won't waste time with small talk, Shiro.

SHIRO: What an astonishing surprise. Are you well?

NESSMAN: What happened at the crime scene?

SHIRO: You know what happened. Do not waste my time.

NESSMAN: I heard from others. I'd like to hear from you.

SHIRO: Which part?

NESSMAN: You arrived shortly before BOFFO staff left the scene.

SHIRO: So? I come to help Cadence occasionally at crime scenes.

NESSMAN: Yes, well, that's the point. It wasn't Cadence who asked you to come.

Chapter Nine

Why had I showed up? Nessman might be an unimaginative bore in Sears suits and bad cologne, but it was a fair question.

One I knew was coming. The man was as subtle as a brick to the frontal lobe. Which just about explains modern psychiatry.

"Shiro? Did you hear me?"

"I have not gone deaf since our last interminable session. She could not see it. I could."

He pretended to doodle. It was shorthand. Old shrink trick. I could read and write shorthand by the time I was six. I could read it upside down by the time I was six and a half. Cadence could not, but occasionally she would glance at Nessman's pad of meaningless (to her) squiggles, which I could decipher later. Her photographic memory came in handy now and again, which almost made up for her cowardly inhibitions.

"Something about the crime scene bothered her. She became upset."

"What was upsetting her?"

Yes, that was the question.

"Shiro?"

"Something about the number three," I muttered, nibbling on a knuckle. I quickly stopped; the knuckle was scabbed and swollen. My sister was up to her old tricks, no doubt. I wondered if she had killed someone. Why was I thinking about her?

"It's not like either of your sisters to disappear out of a crime scene," he was jabbering. Among other things, Dr. Nessman enjoyed sharing facts I already knew. Next he would tell me the forecast called for breezy and seventy-six degrees.

"Cadence is a coward."

"So you say," Nessman said drily. Calculated to make me defend my opinion. That stopped working when I was nine. "Luckily she has you to race to the rescue."

"Ride."

"What?"

"The cliché you are looking for is 'ride to the rescue.'" I eyed his shorthand. *Subject is showing her usual unwillingness to take part in the therapy process. Seems easily distracted.*

Therapy process.

Therapy process.

Process: a procedure; a course; a development.

All words that imply progression.

Subject is showing her usual unwillingness to take part in the therapy process.

Subject thinks you are a douche.

Sure. I have been in the therapy process since I was three.

As far as I could tell, it had not followed any course or developed at all. It just sucked up my Wednesdays.

"I know what you're thinking," Nessman said in what he thought was his soothing voice. It was really his "please hit me in the teeth" voice.

"There are not enough words in English or Japanese to put across how strongly I doubt that."

"We've been talking about this for a while, Shiro."

"Talking about what?"

"Your mother. Your father. What happened when you were three. What happened right in front of you when you were three."

I glanced to the left, eyeing the door. "I have work to do."

"I couldn't agree more. Don't you think you've hidden from the truth long enough?"

"I. Never. Hide."

"Oh, Shiro. We both know that isn't true."

I folded my arms across my chest and stared out the window. The minutes spun by, each one seeming to take at least a week.

"I have mentioned this to you many times," he said quietly. "You—all of you—have plateaued. And you're sitting in that chair thinking this is just a waste of your time."

Damn it. Okay, maybe enough words in English. I seriously considered lapsing into Japanese—Nessman wouldn't know *arigato* from *arrivederci*. But that was a childish refuge, and if nothing else, I prided myself on being more adult and professional than the other two put together. So I decided to stick with English—for the time being.

"We don't have to do anything right this second. If you

would just *consider* integration," Nessman was droning, "open your mind to the possibility, I think your therapy would take a giant step for—"

"No."

"We could just discuss it, Shiro. We don't have to—"

"I said no!"

"And so you see," he said after a long, careful pause, "why therapy can go only so far with you and the others. Integration—"

"Is murder."

It was tough work to shock a shrink—or at least to get one to show it—but I managed nicely with Nessman. He even managed to sound hurt. "Shiro. I would never advocate a course of action that would hurt you, or Cadence, or . . ."

"You are a single; you cannot understand. I acknowledge that you understand our symptoms intellectually, that they can be rolled into a nice easy pack if you do not feel them. You do not *know*. You will never know."

"So explain it to me."

"I have a murder to solve," I replied brusquely, standing. "Really quite a nasty one." Nessman's office wavered around me.

"Sit down, please, Shiro. We haven't finished our session." To his credit, Nessman's voice was firm and didn't cover up edginess. "And of course you do. You're a federal agent. You'll always have a murder, a kidnapping, an Internet scam. You can't hide behind your workload this time."

"I. Do not. Hide."

"Please have a seat, Shiro."

I reluctantly sat, if only to show the man respect: he knew what was inside me.

Who lived inside me.

"You were going to explain that being a single, I can't understand your fear of integration."

"No, that is what you were hoping I would do. *I* was leaving to get back to work."

"But you can't work unless you do this," he reminded me. "It's a condition of your employment. You know that."

Damn it. Rule #1 of BOFFO: weekly psychiatric sessions at a minimum. I could not be sure if this was for our health, since it was not truly in BOFFO's interest for us to get better. Perhaps the legislative committee that quietly authorized our funding needed political cover. In any case, some of us saw a shrink every day. Fortunately, my life had not plunged that far down the toilet.

BOFFO employed sociopaths, like George. Multiples, like my sisters and me. Kleptomaniacs. Pyromaniacs. Agoraphobes. Hysterics. Bipolars. Delusional psychotics. Paranoid psychotics. Schizophrenics. We were surprisingly effective—at least, no one ever complained when budget time rolled around. But of course a large problem was—

"Shiro?"

"What?"

"You were going to explain."

I stared at him as I would at a particularly hairy bug that would not stay squashed. Perhaps that assessment was not fair; Dr. Nessman was rather handsome. Black hair, closely trimmed black beard, sparkling black eyes. Skin the exact color of a good coffee with a splash of cream. And a voice like cabernet—if he hadn't gone into psychiatry he could have been a fine radio personality—smooth and English, just beginning to lose the accent after living and working in Minnesota for over a decade.

"I will not let you kill us."

"Perhaps the others—"

"Feel the same."

I stood and paced a bit; Nessman was used to it and even stretched in his chair a little. It was a nice office: large, with lots of windows. I had a fine view of the U.S. Bank Building, which was an improvement over the garbage-strewn alley below. He could not keep any sculpture in his office, for obvious reasons, but he made up for it in paintings. And Post-its. And doodle pads. And desk blotters. And posters. All featuring ponies. Ponies standing. Ponies running. Ponies playing cards with dogs.

Sometimes I wanted to ask; I never did. He might tell me. More insanity in my life I did not need.

"Three. Why three? And why here, now? Why come to Minneapolis? Always two men and one woman. What is he showing us?"

"He may not know he's showing you anything," Nessman said reasonably. "He may not even know he's doing these things."

I grunted, freshly annoyed. The good doctor did not have to remind me. The ThreeFer Killer was going to be a bitch to hunt (was *already* a bitch to hunt). Most murder victims are killed by someone they know—often, someone they are related to. Most murders are custodial in nature. Serial killers are tough, if for no other reason than that the victims seem to be random.

They are not random. Something about a certain type of

victim sings to serial killers. Gacy liked teenage boys; Bundy liked pretty young women with long dark hair. Our ThreeFer might not know he is being triggered; as Dr. Nessman just said, he might not even know he is running around killing three people per crime scene and dumping them where they will quickly be found. It was this sort of difficulty that caused the FBI to develop ViCAP, the Violent Criminal Apprehension Program, and although I am not the religious type (Cadence is, of all the ridiculous things, Lutheran), I knew it was vital to our work.

"There is just nothing right now," I mused, still prowling the other side of Nessman's desk. "We have reams of paperwork, rooms of files, a thousand pictures per crime scene. We have talked to families, friends, employers, significant others, even parking garage attendants. We have visited homes and their places of employment and their favorite watering holes and bookstores. There is nothing. Not one thing."

"Nice try," Nessman said kindly, "but we aren't here to discuss your latest case, Shiro."

"Why not? It is infinitely more interesting."

"There's only so far I—anyone—can go with you—the three of you—without integration. You were once a whole person, Shiro. You—"

(goose)

"—could be again. Don't you

(Mama look at the goose)

even think about it? You see it

(no Daddy no look out)

as a diminishing, a loss. But

(not the goose you got the goose you)

you're really coming back

(screaming and the blood all the blood and the screaming who's screaming)

to what you once were, what you

(blood on the feathers and I I I we are screaming we are screaming oh won't somebody STOP THE SCREAMING)

were meant to be: a whole person." Dr. Nessman clicked his pen as I turned to face him. "Shiro? What's wrong with your—"

Chapter Ten

Face is stupid, hit it now,
Hit it now, hit it now, while
The wheels on the bus go round and round,
All
        SMACK
                Day
                        SMACK
                                Long.
He can shout all he likes, but I don't care,
I don't care,
Round and round,
The goose won't shut up but I'll make it stop,
Make it stop,
                SMACK
                        Make it stop.
They come in the room and tackle me,
Tackle me, tackle me,
And the goose won't shut up and they tackle me,

Alllllll daaaaay looooong.
"Sedate her!"
Fuck you
Don't you dare
"Come on, sedate her!"
Nuh-uh! Ha!
You'll need more than five
I push off the floor and crush one's nose,
Break another's knee,
Twist another's wrist,
More come in the room and tackle me,
But they won't get me!
They come in the room and tackle me
Allllllll
Alllllll daaaaay . . .
Hey, I guess one got a syringe in after all . . . damn . . .

Chapter Eleven

"What in the world?"

I sat up on a couch I knew well. It was the couch in the waiting area outside Michaela's office, which was completely wrong because I had last been at the ThreeFer crime scene. I had been minutes away from tracking down the family members of our newest victims and starting the long tedious process of twenty questions, times a zillion.

And even if it *was* time for me to be in the building (I peeked at my watch), I should be in my session with Dr. Nessman, not waking up on—

"Oh! Hey! You're awake."

Pam Weinberg, my boss's administrative assistant, was looking at me. Okay, I didn't know that for sure, since she had paperwork, case files, folders, photos, memos, and the like stacked so high that I could see only the improbably orange curls piled on top of her head. There were two phones on her desk, and one of them (often both) rang every two or three minutes.

In a building filled with mysterious government operatives, eyes only/classified documents, and doctor/patient privilege, the biggest puzzle was how seventeen-year-old Pam Weinberg could identify BOFFO members by the sound of our steps.

Uh-huh, really! People lost bets over it. She had ears like a lynx. George once joked that she probably shrieked like a bat so she could navigate office space via sonar.

Although Pam had no line of sight, due to the impossibly tall yet stable stacks of files on her desk, she always knew who was walking in, who was waking up, who was having a nightmare (most of the BOFFO team had ended up on Michaela's couch at one time or another), who was foaming at the mouth, who was late, who was early, who had moved into the waiting room and secretly brushed his or her teeth in Michaela's private bathroom.

Don't look at me like that. I had to live there for only a few days. So I forgot to renew my lease—it's not a crime. Technically, it's a breach of contract.

Well, okay, there was a crime, too. I can feel you judging me. Well, don't. In point of fact, now that I think about it—I did *not* forget to renew, so there. Shiro wrote the check, and then Adrienne jammed it (along with a Spider-Man graphic novel) down the throat of a serial rapist. Oooh, yuck, I can't even think about those crime-scene photos without reaching for an air-sickness bag. The poor guy took almost a year to learn to swallow—and walk—again.

My point is, I had to live in Michaela's office for only six days. So it really wasn't that big a deal.

One thing I sure liked about the waiting room: it was cool, shady, and quiet. The room was about fifteen by twenty, with soft chairs, the aforementioned couch, Pam's desk, and a small fridge in the far corner (always kept padlocked . . . Pam guarded her ginger ale with the zeal of a customs border agent). The carpet was a nice dark blue; the walls were painted the color of a spring sky. The closet had lots of hangers and, on the floor, Pam's sleeping bag, pillow, and neatly folded sushi pajamas.

Oh—sorry. I forgot to tell you. Pam's agoraphobic. I guess she had a pretty crummy childhood, but I don't know any details and I don't want to know. Shiro the snoop does. The only secrets she respects are her own.

So, yes, Pam almost never left the office. She also typed 140 words a minute, never had to be told something twice, kept Michaela's staggering schedule updated, knew who'd been naughty—shoot, she was the perfect palace guard. The fact that she wasn't yet a legal adult was the least important thing about her.

"Are you all right?" Pam asked, fussing with her keyboard. "You've had a busy day."

"Aggh, don't remind me." I looked down. Same clothes as this morning: good. No new stains or dirt: good. A little blood on my knuckles: hmmmm. Almost three hours gone: problematic.

Pam, never one for chitchat, said without looking up from her screen, "You shifted to one sister at the crime scene, and then the other during your session with Dr. Nessman."

"I did *what*?" Appalled, I leaped to my feet. Well, staggered—the trank they must have shot

(her)

me up with was fast acting and, even better, wore off fast. But I'd be wobbly for an hour. "Which sister showed up where?"

"Shiro at the crime scene. You do the math. Speaking of math, you haven't turned in your time sheet for the week."

"Oh my *God*. Oh my God!"

"It's all right. Just get it to me by noon tomorrow."

"Not that. Is Dr. Nessman all right? Is he still here? He's still here, right?" I could feel my face getting hot. Adrienne had never *not* embarrassed me. You couldn't take that girl anywhere. "Did she hurt him? Is he at the ER?"

"I'm sure I don't have to remind you," Pam said drily, and then proceeded to do just so, "but this isn't exactly the first time Nessman's been sucker punched by a patient. Not even that patient. He's fine. He's writing up clinic notes as we speak."

"Oh, I've got to apologize. The poor guy! What happened?" Pam opened her mouth but I rushed ahead. "Don't answer that! Never mind, I don't need to know. I can't believe she—I'll go see him right now. Yes! Right now!"

"You won't, actually." Pam was squinting at a printout of sorts; just another day at the office for her. And me, frankly. "Michaela's waiting for you."

Mental groan. Followed by a verbal groan. Private time with the boss lady. The perfect end to a really poopie day.

"Is she in her office or—"

"The kitchen," Pam answered, already deeply involved with whatever.

The kitchen! She must be having one of those days.

I knew the feeling.

Chapter Twelve

I rapped on the door to the department kitchen and at her absent "Yes, yes" stepped in. Michaela was exactly where I expected her to be—at the counter, chopping celery and cucumbers.

As usual, Michaela presented different sides to different observers. And often, different sides to the same observer. Although she was a late middle-ager, her hair was trendy. Yes, it was silver, but it was cut into a pageboy, the chin-length style you might see on a fifth grader. Her pure green eyes seemed to almost snap with life, but they were bracketed by crow's-feet. Her suit was classic Ann Taylor—which she wore with running shoes. Interestingly, none of us had ever seen her run. I'd never seen her so much as walk fast.

And she was in the kitchen. Not her fancy boss lady office with dark wood and mysteriously locked files. The kitchen!

"Hi." I knew I sounded tentative, but couldn't help it. I hated getting in trouble for something the other two did. Usually people who didn't like their siblings could, oh, what was the phrase? Oh yeah. *Distance themselves from them.* "Uh, hi? How's it going?"

Michaela didn't answer, which was no surprise. She despised small talk almost as much as Shiro did. Judging from the number of bowls she'd set out, it was going to be a Level Four salad. God help us now.

She was scraping chopped celery into a plastic bowl. As always, her food prep was brisk, efficient, and speedy.

Michaela finished, wiped the blade, then stepped to the fridge and rummaged around in the crisper drawer (and woe betide the office intern who put her prized plum tomatoes in the fridge—apparently that ruins their taste). She took out two English cucumbers and began to chop them with one of the several dozen cooking knives she kept in a special set of drawers next to the butcher block—always under lock and key when she wasn't using them.

Not because she was worried one of her clinically insane subordinates would snap and go for a cleaver—we were all authorized to carry firearms, after all. But Michaela was fiercely protective of her brought-from-home Wustof knives.

"What scared you?" Michaela asked, not looking up from her salad prep.

That was chatting with Michaela—by the time she got around to speaking, you forgot why you were supposed to be in there.

I tried to remember. "Well, we were on scene . . . and I saw—I mean, I noticed that the killer might be trying to, uh, send a message."

Michaela arched a silvery eyebrow. "Of course he (or she) is."

"I mean, um. To me. Us, I think. Personally."

Her eyes narrowed. Her chopping sped up. Cucumber slices became airborne before plummeting into an empty bowl. "Us, BOFFO? Or us, you, Shiro, and Adrienne?"

"The latter." Yeesh. Just the thought made me want to crawl into a dark corner of my brain and hide the rest of the week.

"What tipped you?"

"The Three Tenors. The dates on the calendar pages. Variations on the number three. And I'm a triplet."

"A reach," she commented. And she was right. But sometimes you just know. That might seem to make no sense to a layman. But now and again you get a tickle, which leads to a hunch. And the hunch—you know because it feels exactly right. It's like solving a riddle you didn't know you were thinking about.

"Yes," I admitted. "But I'm right. We're right, I mean."

"So. Hmm. The idea frightened you, Shiro came forward to protect you and study the scene somewhat more dispassionately."

"Sure, I guess."

"And then Nessman discussed integration with Shiro—"

"He *what*?" I could feel the color leaving my face. "What's the *matter* with him? Why would he do that?"

"He was tackling the latest item on your agenda to mental health. He did this with my support and approval."

Well, darn. No wonder Adrienne had shot out of my brain and onto the scene. I couldn't blame her. Nobody likes to hear that there really *are* people out to get them. And at work, no less.

"As long as he's okay."

"Indeed." Michaela went to the pantry and extracted two French baguettes. She rinsed and dried the carving knife and put it away, then withdrew a bread knife and began methodically chopping the baguettes into slices. "As I was saying." Chop. Chop. Slash. "Dr. Nessman brought this up during your session with my approval." Cut. Slash. Slice. "And, although unpleasant for everyone, your reaction was expected."

"Oh, well then. Unpleasant for everyone? Gee, that's too bad. Well, as long as no one was taken off guard. Except maybe . . . I dunno . . . me?!?"

"Mmmm. And Shiro certainly came swinging to the rescue, didn't she? Well, that's her function. To help you. To save you. Except she's been doing that too often, we think. Adrienne is showing up more often as well."

I didn't care for the turn in our conversation one little bit. "So?"

Sarcasm, like anything except hard cold data, was lost on my boss. "The other two are manifesting earlier and staying longer. And autumn has rolled around once again—always a bad time for you."

What was she talking about? "What are you talking about?"

"Listen: things cannot go on as they have."

"Huh?" I was right to be puzzled. Can't go on as they have? Autumn? What did back-to-school sales have to do with anything? I'd been this way as long as I could remember. Shiro and Adrienne had always been there. We were a family. A screwed-up murderously nutty family with government benefits and great parking spots.

"You're not a family, you know."

Have I mentioned that when she wasn't julienning carrots, Michaela was a mind reader? At least that was how it seemed to a lot of us.

"I think I know a little bit more about it than you do," I said with more rudeness than was appropriate. Don't judge me! I was shaken up. I can get shaken up and be a little rude once in a while, right?

Right?

"But how could you, Cadence? You've never had what could be called a typical family."

"Then I'm working in the right place, aren't I?" I slumped over on one of the bar stools lining the marble butcher block. "No one at BOFFO could be called a typical anything."

"Your mother killed your father before your eyes when you were three," Michaela went on with terrifying detachment as she hacked a carrot into a pile of orange toothpicks. But if she was trying to rattle me, it wouldn't work—I'd always known that my parents had been, um, unusual.

"You were born and raised on the grounds of the Minnesota Institute for Mental Health."

"Yes, I know all this."

"Most of the residents and half the staff raised you and considered you their own. Your idea of a happy family Thanksgiving is when only two people try to commit suicide before dessert."

"That was just one time," I said hotly, "and who could blame them? They served instant mashed potatoes! You can't expect anybody to suffer through that without consequences."

"And, as I said, Dr. Nessman and I have noted that your alternate personalities have been coming through without being coaxed through therapy. Cadence, do you even remember the last therapy session where you were yourself for the entire hour?"

"Fifty minutes," I mumbled, still steamed that those head-peeping brain-shrinking jerks could call fifty minutes an hour—and sleep at night, too! Not all the crazy people at BOFFO were the field agents.

Look at my boss! Our fearless leader, the one who looked after us and kept us out of trouble and made sure our paychecks came on time and our therapy sessions didn't run over. But she spent an awful lot of time julienning things. Nobody knew why. Not even Shiro! (I think.) But Michaela seemed chilly and well-adjusted only when you put her up against people like me. Or George. Or Opus.

"You are no longer going forward," my (possibly) insane boss continued. "If anything, you appear to be stepping backward. It's unacceptable." Whittle. Chop. Tears were now streaming down Michaela's face, but they didn't fool me—Michaela wouldn't cry if someone dropped a bowling ball on her foot. No, the tears were for the Bermuda onion she was now hacking apart. "So what do you suppose we should do?"

"'We,' you and I? Or 'we,' I, Adrienne, and Shiro?" Big surprise, Michaela didn't answer. "I think you're being pretty mean to them. *You* wouldn't like it if you knew people really were after you."

"People *are* out to get me. . . . I work for the government. And I'm out to get people; that goes without saying."

"I wouldn't say it around here, boss."

"Cadence, I think the three of you need to face the fact that integration *will* happen, no matter how many roadblocks you or the others throw up."

"I can't—"

Chapter Thirteen

"You cannot expect Cadence to face up to that. She never faces up to anything," I said, eyeing the mounds of chopped vegetables with ill-concealed distaste. The woman was the poster child of wasted food. "Expecting her to face facts? What were you thinking?"

"Ah, Shiro, right on schedule." Michaela had made several stacks of bread slices, which she was now bundling into plastic bags and tucking away in the pantry. Her pathology was odd—even for BOFFO—and the irony of her lecturing Cadence about needing to face up to things was not lost on me.

I respected her as I did few others. Yes, I was familiar with her background—I would not work for anyone who kept secrets from me. But, like all of us, she was an asset to BOFFO because of her pathology, not in spite of it. And I kept what I knew to myself—it was nobody's business.

"You're not a moron, Shiro."

"Thank you, I know that."

"None of you are. So you must realize integration is inevitable."

"Of course I do. But expecting Cadence to face unpleasant facts is proof positive that neither you nor Dr. Nessman knows what you are up against."

"Maybe so, but our limits are up to *us*. Not you. Now run along, Shiro."

"Run along?" She did not. She would not dare. Did she just tell me to "run along"? Had I become a child she could dismiss at will?

"I'm giving the three of you the rest of the day off."

"How perfectly splendid," I retorted, then ducked as slices of cucumber got away from her and went sailing over my shoulder. "Never forget—"

Chapter Fourteen

"What?"

Michaela was looking at me expectantly. "Huh?" I asked. "Never forget what?"

"What?"

She slashed the knife through the air with an impatient wave, which made me awfully glad I didn't have male reproductive organs. The men in the office got really nervous when she decided to prep salads, or chop steaks into stew meat. "Never mind. Run home, Cadence. I'm giving you the rest of the day off."

"Really?" I couldn't hide my delight. Today my best friend, Cathie, was (finally!) going to introduce me to her brother. "Okay, great! I'll head out. Thanks."

"We are not finished discussing this."

"For today we are," I said gleefully, crunching across cucumber slices as I headed for the door. Now when had Michaela lost control of the vegetables? And why hadn't I noticed at the time? Oh, who cared. "Okay, see you!"

The crack of the knife slamming through a plum tomato and hitting the cutting board was her good-bye.

Chapter Fifteen

I practically skipped to my cube, snatched up my phone, and punched Cathie's number by memory. As I plopped into my chair I heard the click as she picked up on the second ring, and I launched, too excited for niceties like "Hello."

"You'll never guess. You'll *never* guess! I've got the rest of the day off, so I'm coming over."

"Okay." Hmm. Sounded like Cathie had a heck of a sore throat. She sounded almost masculine. "Who's this?"

Oh. She *was* masculine. I mean, she was a he. "Who's *this*?"

"Oh no. You first."

"Who are you and why are you in my friend's house?"

"Who are you and why are you calling your friend's house?"

"I'm serious."

"So am I."

"Quit that!"

"Okay. I'm here because I lost a bet."

I sat there and tried to figure out if I should be alarmed, irritated, bored, or intrigued. As good gosh is my witness, I hadn't a clue. Cathie was a bit of a loner; in all the time we'd been friends I'd never called her and had a strange man answer. "Um, are you supposed to be there? Is this Patrick?"

"Nuh-uh. You first, I said."

"*I'm* a federal agent. And you're in big big trouble if you're not supposed to be there. Are you?"

"Am I what?" the richly baritone voice asked, sounding equal parts amused and irritated. "Maybe I'm still asleep and this is an unbelievably odd dream. D'you think?"

"I think—" George sauntered by and plopped what appeared to be a ninety-page file on my desk: more gory details from that morning's crime scene. The pictures were prominent and yucky—stabbing victims always looked astonished in death; it was sad and creepy. Think of it: your last memory in life is shock and horror because a big yucky knife is swinging toward your chest. Or throat. Or belly.

Those poor, poor ThreeFer victims, every one of them stabbed and dumped! With nothing in common except an obsessed serial killer who was trying to tell me

(us?)

something. It was so yucky and—and scary—to think that he—that the killer—the ThreeFer Killer—was

(was?)

was—

Chapter Sixteen

He/she was absolutely speaking to me—to us—through his/her victims. I could not say why I was so certain, save that I was and had learned to trust such instincts.

Cadence was a fool—a fool with exquisitely sensitive hunches. Her hunches were a result of input received by all three of us. She could not consciously remember why a memory tugged at her, why a victim or perp seemed to speak to her, but she knew when it was happening, and knew to follow up.

It had saved us on more than one occasion. Except, why was—

"Uh, hello? Mysterious telemarketer?" An unfamiliar masculine voice was buzzing in my ear. "Did you go to lunch? Hello?"

Oh. I was holding a telephone receiver. And, presumably, having a conversation. "Who is this?" I asked sharply.

"Again with that routine? I'm not tellin'. Nope. Not until you do."

"I have no time for this," I said, and disconnected. I grabbed for the topmost file, the one with all the crime-scene photos. It was here, I was certain. All I had to do was—

Answer the phone, which had begun gently buzzing. I snatched the receiver. Perhaps the preliminary lab report had come back—the victims had been at the morgue for hours by now. "Agent Jones."

"*Agent* Jones? That's pretty cool."

"Oh. You again."

"Me again," the stranger replied with nauseating cheer. "I star-six-nined your ass, how about *that*? So who are you and why were you calling my sister?"

"If you are not Patrick Flannery, you are in quite a lot of trouble."

"Even if I am, I'm in a lot of trouble. I forgot I couldn't bring liquids on the plane, so I had to throw away my Gatorade after security made me take off my shoes."

It was entirely possible I was having a conversation with someone not in his right mind.

"Not to mention," he went on with aggravating cheer, "I forgot the charger for my phone, which is currently in my briefcase doing an impersonation of a rock."

"Ah. Well." I could see Tina waving at me from across the room. Damn and damn again! She was likely still looking for that chicken salad recipe for her stupid party. And I, I was trapped like a bug pinned to a board, tethered by this stupid phone conversation.

Never! I would flee, soonest. I needed to find a killer, not swap recipes like a fifties housewife.

Oh, gad, she was coming closer. . . .

Chapter Seventeen

"Hello? Hello? Hello?"

"Huh? Who is this?" I was on the phone, talking to . . . somebody. Oh! And here came Tina. I groped in my top drawer, found the index card with my chicken salad recipe (the secret was olive oil, not mayonnaise, and English cucumbers, not regular ones), and handed it to her as she passed.

"We've been going on like this for a long time," somebody was saying in my ear as I waved to Tina as she hurried away with my precious, precious salad recipe. "I can't tell if I'm intrigued or bored."

"I was intrigued and bored," I said, because apparently Shiro had popped out for a minute or two. "But I've got to go now. I've got the rest of the day—oh, right! Why I called."

"I can't wait to hear this."

"Is Cathie there?"

"So this is Cadence!"

"If you know who I am, then you must be big brother Patrick."

"Guilty," he said modestly, "but it's just Patrick to you."

"It's funny how we've never met before."

"It is?" he asked, then yawned in my ear. "I can think of a lot of things about this situation—"

"What situation?"

"—but funny isn't one of them."

"Listen," I said, striving for patience, "when you see Cathie, tell her I got the rest of the day off, so I'll be over early."

"I'm actually out the door five minutes ago."

"Five minutes ago?"

"I've been having a *weird* conversation with someone who may or may not be Cadence Jones, which is why I didn't leave five minutes ago."

"So?"

"So I'm still here instead of at my lunch meeting. Of course, if I have to choke down one more stale bagel over spreadsheets and P&L reports, I may begin gagging uncontrollably."

"So." I was confused; I admit it. "So you stayed on the phone with me to avoid gagging?"

"It sounds cold when you put it like that," he admitted. "Also, I'm late. Anyway—I'll be back in an hour or so. I'll leave Cathie a note."

"Well. Thanks."

"It's the least I can do. Actually that's not true. I hate when people say that, don't you?"

"Well . . ."

"The least I can do is nothing. So I'll leave a note. The second-to-least thing I could do."

"Great. Well. Bye."

"Bye, Agent Jones."

I hung up and wished I could say that was the oddest phone conversation I'd ever had. But that fight with the dry cleaner on Lake still had first place.

Chapter Eighteen

A word about Cathie, my best friend (but not about her mysterious brother, who is weirdly coy during telephone conversations).

We met at my home, of course, the MIMH (rhymes with "NIMH," as in the Rats of, which is ironic if you think of it) back when we were teenagers and Cathie got a little too carried away with her cutting. Her family thought it was a suicide attempt, so there she was, admitted against her will and forced into, among other unsavory things, group therapy and mass-produced meals (to this day, she can't stand to so much as *look* at Jell-O). I had been at the institute for years when she arrived.

She was as fascinated by my lifestyle ("You live here? You've always lived here? Who takes care of you?") as I was by hers ("Your parents voted Republican? In 2004? How did you manage to hold your head up high, knowing that?"). She was fun and high-strung and creative and deeply moody. Within a year she'd met my two sisters . . . and stayed friends anyway! Once she had done that, I knew she was doomed to be my best friend.

And finally, I was going to meet Patrick. He was ten years older than she was, so she almost never saw him when she was growing up. He was away at college when she started cutting, and only came back to visit a couple times a year, always when I was on the road for work (or seeking new and intriguing therapies). Her parents were both in early-stage Alzheimer's, and Patrick paid for the luxe nursing home they'd been living in for the last six years, ditto Cathie's rent when she couldn't swing it.

He loved his family, I figured, but he didn't know them. Maybe he'd stick around awhile this time.

I headed right to Cathie's from work. She had a beautiful house in Hastings, a town on the Mississippi River. It had been built during the Civil War (the house, not the town), and sometimes I'd find myself looking at the wooden banister or the built-in shelves and think. This was being built while Lincoln was president, while Shiro would think, This built-in shelf was installed the same year Lincoln got shot in the head by a sorry-ass actor, and Adrienne would gouge divots out of the beautifully polished hardwood floor in the dining room. Neat.

I pulled up to her carefully tidy brick house and stepped around the hedges to go to the front door. I liked the woodwork; Cathie liked the hedges. She loved the fact that people couldn't see her even from the front sidewalk. She babied those hedges and practically buried them in Quick Grow. Soon they would reach the second story.

I let myself in—no need to use my key today; she was

shockingly casual about home security—and hollered, "Cath? Where are you?"

Frantic scrubbing was my only answer—ah! The kitchen.

I walked through the living room into her kitchen, where the noise of scrubbing increased. Unfortunately, I couldn't see her, only hear her, which meant—"Cathie, you stop that right now!"

"Stop what?" her voice filtered back, as innocent as a newborn. "Catch any bad guys today?"

"Stop scrubbing that tile with a toothbrush." Have I mentioned that in addition to being a bit bipolar, she also had obsessive-compulsive disorder? "He's your brother, not the pope."

"I wouldn't clean for the pope," she replied—Cathie was that most common of creatures, a lapsed Catholic. "That balding misogynist."

"Nah, I think the new one has plenty of—jeepers, stop scrubbing!"

Cathie slashed at the tile a few more times, but her heart wasn't in it now that I was confronting her, so she stood and dropped the toothbrush in the sparkling clean sink. Her knuckles were pink from pressure, and so were her knees.

It was September, of course, and Cathie would wear shorts or skirts until December 15. Kind of a thing with her. She said winter came only because people believed it would. She was always trying to get other people to dress like it was the Fourth of July during Christmas season. So far, it hadn't worked. The only thing that happened to me was a mild case of frostbite. (Cathie said it was because I wasn't a believer, which is when Shiro told her it was because we were in the

Northern Hemisphere during one of the coldest months of the year. And nearly slapped her.)

Cathie Flannery was a coppery redhead, as the name might have suggested, with fair freckled skin and brown eyes. She was slender and short—she barely came up to my chin. What she lacked in body mass, though, she made up in vitality. Her hugs alone could knock anyone off their feet.

"The house is perfect," I assured her, hoping she wouldn't decide to clean all the bricks with a toothpick dipped in grout. "He'll love it."

"I don't care if he does," Cathie replied, tossing her head so that her hair flew out of her eyes. "I'm cleaning for me, not him."

Sure you are. But I knew better than to say so out loud.

"So!" She perched on the counter and waved her small feet—recently pedicured with orange nail polish, ugh—back and forth. "Anything weird at work? Weirder than usual, I mean. Did your boss julienne potatoes during the morning meeting?"

I giggled. "No, she put it off until the afternoon. I had to help with prisoner transport, and then I caught a crime scene this afternoon, and then I had a session with Dr. Nessman. Shiro did, I mean."

Cathie's eyes went big. "Shiro showed up at work?"

"Adrienne, too," I admitted, glum. No use trying to keep it from Cathie; she always got everything out of me at the end.

"My God! Both in one day! That must have—" We could hear the doorbell echo through the house and she hopped down. "That must have sucked," she said over her shoulder as she rushed to the door. "I want all the gory details later."

I stayed in the kitchen, guessing she'd want privacy to greet the brother she so rarely saw. He was quite a bit older, knew how to bake, and ran his own business—that was all I knew about him.

"Cade, I want you to meet my big brother, Patrick. Patrick, this is my friend, Cadence."

Oh, my. I now knew something else about him, too. He was *gorgeous.*

His hair was such a dark red that it was almost black—you could see the reddish glints if he was standing beside a light source. His eyes, like Cathie's, were a rich chocolaty brown, and he towered over her; I put him at about six foot three. He was dressed in khaki knee-length shorts and a button-down white oxford shirt; his big hairy feet were jammed into a pair of leather sandals.

"Hi," he said, holding out a hand. I was so overcome by his good looks, it took me a couple of seconds to realize I was supposed to shake with him. And when I finally did, I was morbidly aware of my sweaty palms. Why didn't Shiro ever rescue me from humiliation? She only showed when I needed to fight.

"Hi."

"It's nice to finally meet you. My sis talks about you all the time."

I could feel the color rush to my cheeks and looked at my feet. "Oh, well, you know," I said, both self-deprecatingly and idiotically.

"I enjoyed our puzzling yet intriguing phone conversation."

"Uh—oh." This guy? This gorgeous auburn-haired besandaled god had been on the phone with me? And Shiro? *This* guy? "Huh. That's, um, that's nice. And all. Yep."

He grinned, showing the dentition of a soap opera star. "Yep, that's pretty much what our phone conversation was like: puzzling yet weird." He glanced around the kitchen and then turned to his sister. "Cathie, for God's sake. The toothbrush again?"

This forced a giggle out of me, which earned me his bright smile and her glance of dislike.

"So! Who do I have to smack to get some food around here?"

"You're the cook," Cathie snapped. "Why don't you feed us?"

"Ah. The soul of courtesy, no matter what the circumstances. And what kind of a business trip is it if I have to cook?"

Apparently Patrick made a ton of money by baking delicious cakes, pies, and pastries. He certainly didn't look like what I'd imagined a baker to be. He looked like a firefighter who went windsurfing on his off days.

To my amazement, the two siblings were quickly in the middle of a real spat, inching toward each other, gesturing, shouting—soon they would be nose to nose! My God, did she hate him? Did he hate her? Why were they being so mean? Was deep-seated rage the reason they almost never saw each other?

I could do nothing but watch helplessly as the argument escalated.

"—can't just barge—"

"—know who you're—"

"—like to see you—"

Granted, I had no true idea of what constituted "normal family dynamics," but this seemed a little extreme. Soon they would come to blows! I could never let that—

Chapter Nineteen

"Quit that. Right now."

They ignored me and kept shouting at each other. The fools. I eyed the bickering siblings and willed my upper lip not to curl.

It occurred to me that it was getting easier and easier for me to "come forward" and drive Cadence's body. Perhaps that quack, Nessman, was onto something.

But that was not my problem; this was. I seized the siblings by the backs of their necks and briskly banged their heads together. They howled in unison, a grating harmony—his baritone yell, her alto yelp.

"Behave," I said sternly.

Cathie rubbed her forehead, and her eyes widened as she recognized me. "Shiro Jones, you go straight to hell!" she shrilled. "Get out of here! I wanted Cadence to meet my brother. *You* weren't invited."

"Wait," Patrick said, rubbing an identical red spot on his forehead. "What? I thought you said her name was Cadence."

"It *is*. Most of the time, anyway. This is one of her other personalities—Shiro, the one who likes to fight."

"I do not *like* to fight," I corrected her. "But Cadence will not."

"Sure you don't," Cathie replied with uncalled-for rudeness.

While I appreciated Cathie's loyalty to the three of us, I could not help the fact that I did not think much of her. She *cut* her*self*. As if the world were not already full of people who would gladly hurt her for free.

Artists. 'Nough said.

And she did it so she could "feel something." It was puzzling and odd and contemptible. Cadence-the-eternal-ninny was warm and sympathetic. But that was Cadence—always drawn to weakness.

And her older brother, Patrick—I could not deny he was a handsome man. Well built and in decent shape—those weren't health club muscles he was sporting. His skin was a dark tan and his hands were rough—this was a man who spent a lot of time in the open air, who worked with his hands. Not what I would have expected from . . . what was he? . . . right, a baker.

"Jeez," Patrick was saying. "You told me your friend had MPD, but seeing it like this—how about the other one, will she come out, too?"

Cathie and I shuddered in unison. "I hope not," she said, echoing my exact sentiment.

"So the other one—Cadence left because she thought we were going to hurt each other?"

"Yes."

Brother and sister exchanged a look, then burst into laughter. When they did that, I could see their strong familial resemblance and was annoyed to find I was a bit jealous. My family relations were chaotic and weird; all three of us were continually out for ourselves.

"Well, Shiro, we'll be seeing a lot of you," Patrick said. "We've been fighting like this since she started to walk."

"Why?"

"Um, we're Irish?" Cathie volunteered, earning another snort of laughter from her brother.

"So when you were twelve and she was two, you would . . . fight each other?" The wretch.

"Hey, she was the instigator!" the baker yelped. He pulled up a sleeve and showed me a pink scar on the underside of his wrist.

"That looks like—"

"It is! She freakin' *bit* me! Not out of diapers for a year and she chomped me like a T-bone."

"Suck it up, crybaby," Cathie said, admirably unashamed.

"You should see all the other scars I've got."

"Perhaps another time." Or perhaps never. "Behave yourselves. In case it has escaped your notice, I am trying to catch a serial killer."

"Of course it escaped my notice," Patrick replied. "How the hell would I *know* that?"

A rather good point. Why had I said such a thing in the first place? I—I was not trying to impress this handsome, handsome man. Was I?

Was I?

Cathie smacked him on the meaty part of his upper arm. "I told you. She works for the FBI."

"Is nothing sacred?" I cried. And I might have asked Cadence-the-blabbermouth the same thing. She knew our work was confidential.

Which did not excuse my own babbling.

So I fled.

Chapter Twenty

I blinked, almost feeling the silence. "What?"

Cathie and Patrick were staring at me, though I hadn't said anything. I knew that look, though, and peeked at my watch. About two minutes, gone.

"Oh nuts." I groaned. It'd be nice if once, just *once,* Shiro or Adrienne would warn me before she took over the driver's seat. "Are you all right? I'm sorry. But jeepers, I was kind of worried you'd really hurt each other."

"Jeepers?"

"Cadence doesn't ever swear."

"No shit?"

"She leaves that to Adrienne," Cathie added.

"You're just full of helpful tidbits today," I snapped.

"Oh, the other one," Patrick said, and to his credit, he looked interested, not horrified. Still, I wanted to hide in a cupboard.

"I can't believe you—you *told* him about us?"

"Well, sure." Cathie was sounding perfectly reasonable, like she'd given him a recipe for stock. "He's my brother. We talk."

"Can't you just complain about your parents or local sports teams?" I whirled on Patrick. "Don't judge me!"

His hands shot into the air as if he were being held up. "Never! I stick with judging my nutjob little sister."

I laughed—I couldn't help it—and Patrick continued. "I'd hate to meet any of you in a dark alley, frankly."

"It probably won't be a problem. Ugh, okay. I've been here long enough. I'm going home," I muttered, looking around for my bag. "It's been a very long, very weird day."

"Yes, I can see how all this would be stressful. For *you,*" Patrick added, but his dark eyes were—was that a twinkle? It was! I didn't think there was such a thing outside of books.

"You just—never mind."

"Don't you have a hot date with that Detective Clapp?"

"I do indeed. So farewell, *arrivederci,* buh-bye, whatever."

"Give him a kiss for me," Cathie called after me as I slung my schlep bag over one shoulder. "With lots of tongue."

"And me," Patrick added, which made me grin in spite of myself.

So, yeah. It was safe to say that I liked him from the start.

Chapter Twenty-one

"You look terrible."

"I feel terrible," I admitted.

George and I were heading out for some routine interviews to follow up on the latest ThreeFer killing. He had been out most of the morning—"sick" he said, but I suspected just staring at himself in a mirror, trying to figure out the most perfectly awful tie. He was driving; I just wasn't up to the argument it would take to get him out from behind the wheel.

"You want to get something to eat?"

"I'm not hungry."

George said nothing for another mile or so. Then, as we sat at a red light and he drummed his fingers on the steering wheel, he asked, "You should probably eat. I didn't see you eat anything yesterday."

"Just because you didn't see me eat doesn't mean I didn't. I have a life beyond the office, George."

"No. You don't." Not saying it in a mean way.

Huh. Usually when I was upset about something George

encouraged Shiro or Adrienne to come out and keep him company while I, to use his compassionate phrase, "quit having a friggin' poopie."

"That's not true."

"It is, actually."

"Is *not*!" I straightened so quickly I nearly strangled myself on the shoulder belt. "I'm—I've met someone." Uh. I was pretty sure.

"That's better," George said, yawning so widely I could see his fillings. "Conversation is good, even if it's about a guy you're not even dating yet. You've *met* him? That's it? He could be a door-to-door salesman, I guess. Fuck, you're killing me. Though I suppose this is an improvement over sitting in that passenger seat like a wordless blob. That whole pissing and moping about your condition gets *really* boring."

"Sorry, George. I should have realized how difficult this was. For *you*."

"Well, Cadence, I didn't want to have to say so, but yeah, that's exactly right."

"I really, really hate you."

My partner laughed. "Sorry, Pollyanna. You absolutely don't. You don't hate anyone—which is part of your problem."

"Thanks for the analysis, Freud." And what had gotten into the poster pinup for amorality? He sounded almost—what was the word . . . uh . . . interested? No. Concerned! George sounded *concerned*. About me. Good gosh. The entire planet was imploding around me. "Now, if you don't mind, why don't we—gaaah!"

I'd "gaaahed" because George had slammed on the brakes and, for the second time in twenty seconds, I'd nearly been strangled. There was a thud as we went up on the curb, a click as he disengaged his seat belt, and then the door was open and he was running away.

I struggled free of my own seat belt, grabbed his keys, and climbed out. At least he hadn't run anyone over this time, thank goodness, but that trash can was never going to be the same again. It was wedged under the left front wheel.

"George! What the heck?" I glanced around at the witnesses on the street. "Uh. Official business, everyone. Nothing to see here." Nope. Nothing—not a government-issue vehicle on the sidewalk outside Murray's steak house, the pulverized trash can, my partner sprinting off into the distance like the hounds of heck were on his butt, and me yelling after him, minutes or perhaps seconds before switching personalities. Happens all the time. "Well, okay. There's plenty to see here, but it's rude to stare."

"D'you need an ambulance?"

No, just a shrink. And maybe a tow truck.

"Wow!" A boy in a Timberwolves jersey which fell to his blue-jeaned knees was pointing at me. No. Past me. "Look at *that* guy!"

I looked. Then I scrambled across the hood of our steaming, hissing government-issue vehicle and ran after George as fast as I could.

Chapter Twenty-two

"Don't touch them, George!" I shrieked, knowing I was going to be too late, knowing I wouldn't be able to stop my partner, and also that I was going to have a terrible sore throat in the morning. "The restraining order is still in effect! You are well within fifty yards! And we're illegally parked!"

I nearly tripped and went somersaulting over a newspaper machine and thought, This is a huge waste of time. I'd sure like to have the last thirty seconds of my life back. Also, it'd be swell if I could go one day this month without falling, choking, crying, seeing a shrink, seeing another ThreeFer crime scene, and—oh yes! Without having to chase someone and bring him down like a dang gazelle!

Thank goodness street traffic—both auto and pedestrian—was low today. Smashed-up innocent bystanders I didn't need.

One had gotten past George, and as he streaked by on my left, I shouted, "FBI! Haaaaaaands!" again, for all the good it did. I couldn't catch this one and help George with the others, so my order was mostly bluff.

"Hey, that guy—"

"—the car just flew up on the—"

"—garbage can!"

Darn it! Dang it! Dump it! Yes, I *know* I'm close to swearing, and guess what? I think I'm entitled to toss around a few vulgarities. The raggety-blamed stress was darn near killing me.

Just about when I was about to give up, one of the men George had been chasing blasted out of the alley in front of me holding—would this day never end?—a tire iron. Within two seconds, he saw my badge and decided his best course of action was to take a

Chapter Twenty-three

Swing wide

Sweeeet chariot

Turn those wheels and carry me home!

Bad day to be you.

Silly.

Goose.

Chapter Twenty-four

I awoke to find the unconscious—and possibly dead—body of David the Duke (birth name: Tyrone Lee; DOB: 4/4/82) at my feet. He was a sprawl of dirty and bloody denim, strappy and bloody T-shirt, and steel-toed and bloody boots.

Ah, there, one of the boots moved. Less paperwork. Excellent.

I turned to look for George. The two men he was chasing were, if my partner's past actions were any indication, destined for colostomy bags and exploratory surgery. Not to mention all the weeks of physical therapy.

Sure enough, as I explored the alley two blocks away, I began to hear a familiar voice, punctuated by pounding sounds.

"Huh? Do *you* like people hurting *you* for something *you* can't help? Huh? Huh?"

I had to admit, I was almost impressed. George's fists were a blur; each "huh?" was punctuated with another blow. It sounded like he was punching hamburger. Which, in a way, he was.

"How about I cut that swastika off your arm and make you eat it? Huh? Huh?"

We were likely going to be here for a bit, if for no other reason than we would have to call an ambulance for each of the pulverized skinheads and then wait for the sirens. And I had no intention of putting a stop to any of it. It was more therapeutic than hypnosis, and infinitely more interesting to watch.

"You get that this just proves to everyone that you're a closeted fag, right? Right? How about *that*?" There was a crunch as George broke Don Black's nose. Two against one—that was hardly fair when you were up against someone as ruthless as my partner.

"Because if you *don't* like it, then why the *hell* do you keep beating up homosexuals?" Thwack. Thud.

George was never going to get those stains out of his suit.

"Don Black?" Whump. "Kevin Strom?" Whu-thud. "And your other fellow Nazi, the one who got past me. David the Duke, you pathetic closeted anti-Semitic bag of shit? You formed your little club and named yourself after a bunch of ignorant crackers. *Most* of whom were too stupid to stay out of prison—that is, when they weren't filing fraudulent income tax returns."

I pulled up a pack of cigarettes I had bummed from David the Duke—he was not using them, after all. I cracked it open, found two inside with a lighter, took one, lit the cigarette with the lighter, and took a deep inhale. I was not a regular smoker, but now and again I found the occasional cigarette to be soothing.

"Hey, Cadence?" A yowl of pain from Kevin Strom as

George seized his testicles and twisted. "You got anywhere to be in the next half hour?"

"Shiro. And no." I flapped a hand at him, smoke trickling out of my nostrils. "Take your time."

"Hear that, scumbag? The one person at work who's crazier than I am thinks I should take—my—time!"

"I beg your pardon. I am certainly not the one person at work crazier than you."

"Oh, cram it up your ass, Shiro!"

I took another drag, idly wondering about what never failed to set George off. Not only was he amoral and conscience-free, he was not gay or Jewish. Neither was anyone in his family, by his own admission. And yet he had, figuratively speaking, many many homophobic and anti-Semitic scalps on his belt.

Mysteries, mysteries.

"Have you looked in a mirror lately, you cowardly puke? How many teeth do you even have left? The average IQ score in your pathetic gang is 112 and none of you made it past the middle of your junior year in high school."

I took the cigarette out and studied it. Cadence did not smoke. Finding a cigarette in her hand would upset her. Smelling the smoke—tasting it in her mouth—that would upset her, too. Not in a traumatic sort of way, to be sure. But it would still be deeply irritating.

"The master race?" A bubbly moan. "Give me a break! No, never mind, I'll give *you* one." There was a final crunch, and then silence.

I puffed and waited.

George hurried out of the alley and stalked past me, muttering under his breath. His dark hair had flopped into his eyes. His green eyes—interesting, the strangest people I knew all had green eyes, hmm—were slits of extreme piss-off. His face was spattered brow to chin in a fine red spray of what I took to be back-splatter, probably arterial. His suit jacket looked like he'd dipped it in red paint before leaving the alley. His tie, which had a pattern of turtles split in two swimming in bloody soup, had real patches of crimson on it.

"That was nicely done, George. Your punches are getting more economical all the time."

"Go to hell."

I took the cigarette out of my mouth, studied it, thought about discarding it, and then had a truly wicked idea. I sucked in one last puff and fell into step behind the Anti–anti-Semitic Avenger. "Michaela will be annoyed."

"I give a shit."

"No. You do not. Really, George, in front of civilians? On a city street? There are only a hundred ways to do what you do without getting caught—and you know every one of them."

"Maybe it's not about not getting caught."

"Oh, quite possibly." I was not sure where George thought he was going; our car was still hissing on the curb, and at the least, we needed a tow.

Either way, playtime was over.

Chapter Twenty-five

"***Iuugh!* KACK! Oh** my good—KACK—jiminy gosh!" I coughed and spit and then coughed again.

"Knock it off," George snapped, and I was shocked at his appearance. He looked like he'd gone ten rounds with the Rock's stunt double. He looked, in other words, almost as bad as our car did. That would be the third car he or I had totaled in five weeks. (Though to be fair, Adrienne had totaled the last one; I was but an innocent.)

"Rrrggghh. Oh. Oh my goodness. Ick . . ." I bent at the waist and nearly barfed all over my shoes. What the—my—what the *hell* was a *cigarette* doing *in my mouth*?

"Oh that wretch! That fiendish rotten—" Words failed me. I spit the cigarette out and then scrubbed my tongue with my fingers. My mouth tasted like an ashtray after a sparrow spent the weekend pooping in it.

This was Shiro's idea of a joke, that hard-hearted shrew. Like Adrienne, she got bored if she stayed too long; unlike

Adrienne, she could plan. Sisters' tricks on each other were not always kind.

"I don't smoke!" I raged, almost running after George. "But what will you bet I'll have to deal with the lung cancer issues, huh? Huh? Who is dumb enough to smoke these days? I could have been burned! I could have aspirated on my vomit and died! I could have—uh—nicotine-stained fingers! Oh, rats, my mouth." I untucked my shirt and scrubbed at my tongue with my shirttail. "Do they still make Topol? I'm not going to use Topol!"

"Brush your teeth with strawberry douche, see if I care. Come on."

"Well. That wasn't very nice at all, you know, and—George?" Wow, he was really putting some distance between us. I had seen him like this only on the day the little group of skinheads he'd spent nineteen months tracking down were acquitted of murder charges. Oh boy. He hadn't been able to get the blood out of his carpet and ended up moving to a new place—*and* losing his security deposit. Shiro (of all people!) had helped him move to his new condo near Riverplace.

"George? Hey, wait up! I'm not doing all this paperwork, you know. You made the mess; *you* fill out the forms. And get Michaela to sign off on them. And the next time Shiro sticks anything tobacco-related in *my* mouth, could you kindly bust her in the ribs?"

With a final, defeated retch, I managed to recover from my near-death experience and hurried after my partner.

Chapter Twenty-six

We got a cell call as we jumped into a taxi. Federal agents, hailing a cab—nothing like a fresh humiliation in the middle of the workweek. What we heard was even worse news than Shiro's long-term plan to kill me with lung cancer.

There was *another* ThreeFer crime scene. Two in twenty-four hours? Awful, awful to contemplate. This wasn't escalation; it was lunacy. What the heck was going on?

We were told where to go and we promised to get there pronto. I groaned inwardly because I'd have to cancel my date with Jim Clapp. I knew he'd still be at the Cop Shop, so I dialed his direct number.

"Homicide, Clapp."

"Hi, it's me."

"Cadence?"

"Yeah, listen—I've got to hit a scene. I'm afraid I'm going to have to cancel."

A perplexed silence on his end; I was about to repeat myself, louder and slower, when he said, "But you already canceled our date."

"What?" When had *that* happened? I realized Shiro must have done it when she came forward at the earlier scene. Drat that girl! She had a lot of nerve, canceling *my* dates. I didn't cancel hers! Not that she'd had a date since . . . uh . . . hmm. "I mean, uh, right. Right! But maybe we can reschedule."

"Uh-huh," Jim replied, sounding puzzled and amused. "Sure. Call me whenever."

I disconnected the call and glared at my reflection in the taxi's backseat window. "If you can hear this," I muttered, "you stay out of my dating life, you hear me, sis? Just stay *out*."

There wasn't an answer. Not that I'd been expecting one.

I sighed. The taxi driver shifted into third and put the hammer down. Traffic was light, so we would get to the new scene in just a few minutes.

Chapter Twenty-seven

We pulled up outside a steak house in South Minneapolis with the amusing name of the Strip Club.

We saw the taxi off, flashed our IDs at a clearly amused uniform, and joined her in the doorway. "Is it?"

"Looks like."

"Two in one day?"

"Yup. Pretty nasty in there." The uniform, Officer Baylor, a trim brunette with big dark eyes and the cheekbones of royalty, shook her head. "Luck."

"Thank you, Off—"

George swore in the middle of my gratitude. "He's clearly escalating, the jerkoff. I had tickets to Jim Gaffigan, damn it!"

"Escalating?" Officer Baylor asked. That was too mild a word, kind of like describing the sun as "shiny."

I guess I better hold up a sec and explain. The more serial killers kill, the more they want to kill. It's like getting high. The first couple times you smoke or snort or whatever, it's more than enough. But eventually, you have to do more and more of your drug of choice to get back that first, intense high.

Serial killers are no different. They can start out killing one or two victims a year . . . and then every six months . . . every month . . . every week. It proved to be the downfall of several of them, notably Ted Bundy and John Wayne Gacy. Escalation led to sloppy thinking and worse.

Now here we were with two crime scenes in one day.

Two crime scenes in the city where I lived and worked.

This was the best time to catch serial killers. They weren't as careful. They made mistakes. Too bad that the whole time they were being careless, the body count was racking up like pins in a bowling alley.

One of the problems with escalation is that it doesn't work. It's not a quick cure; it's not any kind of cure at all. It merely makes everything worse. So the killer—honestly puzzled by this—takes more lives. And is enraged and confused when that doesn't work, either.

It's important, if difficult, to keep in mind that serial killers honestly feel cheated out of what's theirs. That the cops have no business messing in their private lives. As Ann Rule put it in the awesomest true-crime book ever, "What Ted Bundy wanted, Ted should have." So glad I didn't have to work any of his crime scenes; may his soul be shrieking in hell for a million zillion years.

They don't stop trying, either. They really think that if they can kill just the right person, they can be normal. Be *real.* If it weren't so awful, I could feel sorry for them. But it is awful, and I don't.

"We caught a break, though," Baylor was saying. "There's a live victim."

"What?" Try as I might, I couldn't keep my jaw from sagging. "Are you kidding?"

"She'd better not be," George offered. "I never kid when I'm forced to miss Jim Gaffigan. D'you know I bought these tickets over six months ago?"

"The victim, George. Focus, please."

"Yeah, yeah."

Baylor continued. "She locked herself in the pantry while our adorable li'l ThreeFer was going to work on victims one and two."

"Is she hurt?"

"She says not, but she won't come out."

"Does she know I have Jim Gaffigan tickets?"

Officer Baylor merely stared at George, a not uncommon reaction.

George prodded me. "Go on in, Cadence. Work your good-girl magic." He managed to say this without gagging, luckily for him. "I'll stay out here and—Nance!" Baylor and I jumped as George shrieked loudly enough to shatter windows. "I see you over there, Nance! Turn out your eight zillion pockets now!" Jerry backpedaled, alarmed, as George marched over to him.

"You guys." Officer Baylor was certainly getting an eyeful today. "You, uh, have your own way of doing things, huh?"

I shrugged. "So, you want to show me?"

"Sure."

So Shiro fights. And Adrienne hurts. Me? I am good at

talking to people. I love to talk to people. Which has come in handy on more than one occasion.

Like now! Oooh, I couldn't wait to talk to the poor thing. Finally, finally, finally a break.

I fell into step behind the officer, catching a few glimpses of body bags and the ME, Dr. Gottlieb. She was crouched over a zippered bag, stripping off her gloves and tossing a casual wave in my direction.

Officer Baylor led me to the kitchen and showed me the (locked) pantry door.

"It locks from the inside?"

Officer Baylor nodded.

"Why would somebody want to lock herself inside a pantry?"

"You mean, besides avoiding the psycho hacking people up in the dining room?"

"Well. Yes. Besides that. Never mind, Officer, I'll take it from here. What's her name?"

Baylor shrugged, tugged off her hat, and ran her fingers through her short brunet hair. "She won't say."

"Oh. Okay, thanks." Yes, you've been *loads* of help, Officer; don't know what I'd have done without you. I better not say it out loud, though. Being surrounded by death and blood and misery (not to mention Dr. Gottlieb's perfume) was no excuse for being mean.

I rapped on the pantry door while around me the hustle and bustle of crime-scene processing went on. "Ma'am? My name is Special Agent Jones; I'm with the FBI. Can I speak with you?"

"Go away!"

"I can't, ma'am." My partner wrecked our car and our cab

left two minutes ago. Hmm. Prob'ly should keep that to myself. "Are you hurt?"

"What if he comes back?"

"Then my partner will shoot him in the face," I promised. It wasn't a lie, either. George considered a day without a civil rights violation the worst sort of lost opportunity.

Silence. Then, "*You* come in. By yourself."

"Sure. D'you have any crackers in there? I skipped lunch."

Another pause, broken by the snick of the lock being disengaged.

I stepped inside and prepared myself to meet the first live victim after more than a dozen attacks.

Date? What date? Now I was glad Shiro had canceled for us. Maybe I'd leave her a thank-you note somewhere.

Or not.

Chapter Twenty-eight

The pantry was cool and dry and well lit, with shelves of dry goods going back at least eight feet. The as-yet unnamed victim was crammed as far away from the door as she could get—understandably.

I flashed what I hoped was a friendly and sympathetic (but professional—mustn't forget that) smile. "Hi. I'm Cadence Jones. You're having an awful day, aren't you?"

The victim, a dark-haired, brown-eyed woman of average weight and (I was pretty sure) height, made a sound halfway between a bark and a giggle. She looked like she was in her late forties, but my estimate could be off by as much as ten years, depending on what the stress of the day had done to her face. "You could say that."

"D'you mind if I sit?"

She shook her head, further messing up her hair, which had probably been pinned back in a neat bun when she left her home that morning. Now it fell around her face in dark straggles.

I sat cross-legged across from her. My gun dug into my hip and I grimaced and moved it over an inch.

"D'you want to tell me . . ." Everything? What happened? What did he look like? Why did you survive? Did you know the other two victims? Tell me tell me tell me *every single thing.*

Whoa. Calm down, Cadence. I tried to get a grip on myself. The *last* thing I needed was Shiro thinking I needed rescuing. She was a disaster at interpersonal relations, and would scare this poor woman worse than she already was.

I took a deep, steadying breath and asked, "Can you tell me your name?"

"Tracy. Tracy C-Carr."

"And how did you come to be here tonight, Ms. Carr?"

"Dinner. I was supposed to meet a blind date." She laughed, the sound not unlike breaking glass. "Everybody knows blind dates aren't any fun, but I never dreamed—I never thought—"

"Sure, sure. Prob'ly would have been a good night to watch reruns, or empty out your TiVo account."

A ghost of a smile, gone so quickly I wondered if I'd imagined it.

"So you came here to meet a date . . . ," I prompted, already needing to find out who set her up, whom she was supposed to meet—a thread which might turn into nothing. Or everything. Puzzle pieces, puzzle pieces . . .

It was so great to have a live victim. I vastly preferred chitchat to meetings in the morgue. We needed to find out everything about her—who she was, where she lived. Her job. Her friends, her family, her boss. Her blind date. Her family physician, her minister, her book club. Her dry cleaner, her car wash, her Jiffy Lube. Her grocery store, her vacation plans, her pets. Same old, same old—but we were getting there. I knew it. I think the others did, too.

"And then—and then I was in here, calling 911 on my cell phone."

I blinked. Surely not another woman who lost time. Of course, trauma could certainly account for her not remembering the actual attack.

"So you called for help . . ."

"And I waited." Her big eyes were shiny, almost glassy. Shock, of course. She was either in it or getting there. "And then—then I could hear the police. And then you were knocking on the door."

Nuts. A memory gap of at least forty-five minutes. Well, maybe there'd be something on her clothes, under her nails. Caught in her hair. In her purse. On her iPod. Anything. Puzzle pieces, puzzle pieces . . .

"Well, Ms. Carr, I'm going to ride along with you to the hospital. We'll have a guard on your door 24/7." I hated how overused those numbers were, except when it was the literal truth. Ms. Carr wouldn't be blowing her nose unobserved for the next several days. "We'll get you checked out, make sure you—you're okay. Do you want me to call somebody?"

"No."

Definitely distant. Pulling away from reality. Boy, could I relate.

"Ms. Carr?"

"Mmm?"

"We'll get him."

She blinked at me slowly, like an owl. "Promise?"

"Oh, yes."

Her lips trembled and she was finally able to force out, "Thank God. Thank God for that."

God? Prob'ly not. BOFFO, though. They'd do the trick.

We would, I mean.

Chapter Twenty-nine

The next morning I lurched out of bed (I woke up alone, thank goodness) and staggered to the bathroom. What with processing the scene, escorting Tracy Carr to the hospital, going back to the office and filing paperwork, I'd been home for only about—

I peeked at my watch and groaned. Three hours. Ugh. I badly wanted more sleep. Or at least a long, hot bath. Unfortunately, it was the second Tuesday of the month.

Oh—right. I forgot you didn't know. Cathie and I have been having breakfast at the Eagan Perkins once a month for the last ten years. With her traveling schedule and my career, if we didn't have a set place and time, whole months could go by without us hooking up. Thus, the second Tuesday of the month was inviolate unless it was something important, like arresting a killer or needing stitches, or really really bad menstrual cramps.

So imagine my surprise when I walked into the restaurant to find Patrick—and only Patrick—at our table.

"Eh?" I said.

"Articulate even at such an obscene hour," the baker said, closing his magazine (*People's Most Fascinating People*) with a brisk snap. "Marvelous."

My, my. He certainly was a handsome one. I could see him from only the waist up, but he was wearing what I suspected was a designer suit. It didn't have that boxy look that bespoke retail.

And that grin! Those eyes!

Get a grip, Cadence. Right, okeydoke. "Where's Cathie?"

"Ah. The eternal question. Where *is* Cathie?"

I slid into the booth and resisted the urge to peek under the table to check out the rest of his suit.

"My darling little sister got a phone call yesterday evening—another one of her paintings sold, and the gallery owner wanted her downtown pronto to discuss another show."

"Golly! That's great." Cathie was, among other things, a ridiculously talented artist. She made Picasso look like a kindergarten finger painter. Me personally, I always got a headache when I looked at her work too long, but it definitely appealed to certain groups. (Case in point, Adrienne.) I probably just wasn't deep enough to really get her work; I'll be the first to admit, me not know nothing 'bout art.

My favorite was a huge canvas, eight feet by six, liberally splashed with vibrant purple and blue, smeared with indigo, and splattered with red dots. She called it *The Face of Love,* whatever the heck that meant. To me it looked like a big old brightly colored mess. Which is why I caught bad guys and Cathie painted things like *The Face of Love.*

"Alas, she knew you were on scene—I assume that's a nod

to your crime fighting, and not that you're an actress—and wanted to make sure you knew why she was so callously blowing off your monthly Perkins breakfast of runny eggs and burnt hash browns."

"Crime fighters are actresses," I said, "and the hash browns aren't burnt. And thanks for the cupcakes."

The cupcakes! I'd been toiling over paperwork last night when a messenger was cleared to my floor bearing a delivery for yours truly. It turned out to be half a dozen devil's food cupcakes frosted with lush, creamy buttercream frosting, each a different pastel shade. They looked like Easter eggs and smelled like Godiva. I'd nearly swooned right into the pastry box. And had gobbled down four of the six before having to call a halt due to an encroaching sugar-induced fit of frenzy.

" 'Twas nothing," he said modestly, but looked pleased. "Cathie warned me you had hideous eating habits, that sometimes you skip meals for days in a row. I thought about sending you a salad, but where's the fun? It's salad."

"They were great." I was still puzzled—why would he send sweets to someone he'd just met? Well. He was probably just a very nice man. I reached for a menu I'd memorized almost a decade ago. "And my hash browns aren't burnt, they're crisped."

"You say tomato, I say burnt. But back to our featured story: I, her trusty older brother, rode in on—"

"An SUV hybrid."

"Yes, that's—wait. How'd you know what I was driving?"

"Because I work for the government, silly. I know all kinds

of things. Supersecret things." (Also, Cathie had mentioned a few months back that her brother was getting downright smug about all the gas he *didn't* have to buy.)

"Okay. Well, my SUV and I are here to treat the lady to breakfast. Any of the ladies," he added.

"You really don't know what you're talking about," I said kindly. "And I find it a little odd to be discussing family members—not to mention MPD and psychoses—with someone I've known less than twenty-four hours."

"I bring that out in gorgeous blondes."

I rolled my eyes—was it me, or was I hip deep in manure and still sinking? "I'm amazed Cathie told you anything."

"What?"

"I'm amazed Cathie—"

"Sorry, 'what' in this case meant incredulity, not 'speak up, I'm losing my hearing.' Why?"

"What?"

"Is that 'what' a request for more information, or—"

I scowled at him. The conversation, which had been going on for only two minutes, was already exasperating me. Hmm. Guess they really *were* brother and sister.

"Didn't you know, Cadence? Cathie talks about you all the time."

"Nuh-uh!"

"Yuh-huh. You're in every letter and e-mail and LiveJournal entry she ever sent me. She adores you. Didn't you know that?"

"She does? How come? She's the really talented one. She spends her days creating art out of nothing."

"Whereas all you do is stop serial killers from racking up the body count. My, my, how do you live with the horror? It's so *odd* when a woman has no idea how wonderful she is."

And he reached across the table, picked up my right hand, and kissed the tips of my fingers.

Chapter Thirty

I yanked my hand back—gently, let's not bruise Cathie's brother just yet—and leaned back in the booth. I could feel my face getting red. I wasn't sure how to feel at all. Or, rather, I was feeling everything at once.

I was embarrassed that a mysterious baker knew so much about me. I wasn't exactly unthrilled that he was showing interest on short acquaintance. I was a little ticked at Cathie for her indiscretion while at the same time I was wildly flattered that she held me in such high esteem.

And the thing was, if Cathie hadn't met me on the grounds of my childhood home, the institute, I never would have told anyone. But we formed a bond almost immediately, and best of all, she observed the antics of my sisters and never made me feel bad, or crazy. She knew my secrets before we needed training bras, as I knew hers. Secrets, that is. For all I knew, she still wore training bras. (Meow!)

I had told her about the girls long before I went anywhere near Quantico. But that didn't mean I wanted her whole family in on my deeply personal emotional problems. Although I wouldn't mind if Patrick wanted to kiss my fingertips again. That had been different. Heck, my hand was still tingling.

"Anyway," Patrick continued cheerfully, "I jumped at the chance to finally meet you."

I was amazed. "That's why you came out here from Boston? Just to meet me?"

"No, I also needed to talk to a few new investors."

"Investors?"

"Sure, for my business." He laced his hands behind his head and talked to the ceiling. "I oversee about twenty thousand pastries a week, but I'd like to get a partner or two to help share the load."

"Share the load?"

"Sure. We just acquired a competitor last month."

"Who's that?"

"Homemade Goodness."

I gasped. "I love Homemade Goodness. They make the best . . ." Then I had it. Patrick was . . . Auntie Jane's Cakes and Pies? "You're Auntie Jane! Oh, gosh! You're *famous*; I buy one of those things practically every week—say! That's why you have a meeting—you're probably going to talk to the head of another grocery chain and get a few thousand more cookies stocked each week."

"Yeppers. But I'm not surprised Cathie didn't tell you I was the head of a chain; she hates corporate America. So she introduces me as a baker. Which, of course, I am."

This actually made sense. Cathie grew up with money, enough that she barely noticed if someone else was rich. It was very much in character for her to dismiss her brother's vast personal fortune.

Is it just me, or do the people who don't care about money hardly ever need it, while people who do care about it never get it? A puzzle for the ages.

"Well, that must be nice. Being your own boss and such."

"Yeppers."

Have I mentioned how difficult it was for me to find dates who wouldn't care about my MPD? By the time I felt comfortable enough to explain, the date du jour either didn't care, or was long gone, or had judged me. And don't get me started on intraoffice dating—talk about a recipe for disaster!

It was both nice and nerve-racking to run into a fella who knew about my eccentricities from the get-go.

I told that to Auntie Jane, who grinned and replied, "You don't scare me, Cadence Jones. I've lived with crazy, I've ridden with crazy, I've vacationed with crazy, I've visited crazy in various hospitals, I've sat in on therapy sessions with crazy. Frankly, I think women who don't have major emotional disorders are really very dull."

"Then you're going to love me," I said drily.

"Oh, I'm counting on it. Ah, the waitress cometh. Know what you want?"

"It's a pretty long list. Oh, breakfast! Sure."

I ordered my usual; Patrick, who apparently burned calories at the speed of light, ordered a tall pancake stack swimming in maple syrup.

"So. When can I meet the rest of the family?"

"Huh?"

"You know. Your family."

"Uh. Well. Ahm." I could feel myself getting decidedly nervous. I didn't like to talk about my late parents. I didn't like to talk about much at all from my years on institute property. "There's, uh, not much to tell."

"Oh, I'm sure that's not true."

"Let's just eat our breakfast."

"But it hasn't arrived," he pointed out.

"Let's just eat, okay?"

"Cadence, if it seems like I'm prying, then I apologize. I'm just curious about you, that's all. There's nothing to—"

I raised my hands above my head and slammed both fists on the table, hard. *"I do not want to talk—"*

Chapter Thirty-one

Pillsbury Doughboy, now you see,
Now you see
Now you see
The wheels on the bus go round and round
All
        Day
                Long!

But Baker I like that you asked for me
That you wanted to see
        See!   See!
                Me!
So I won't hit you now, hit you now, hit you now
(But maybe later, Pillsbury!   Yesyes!)

Here comes the waitress
With your syrup
Round and round

And I grab the syrup
Round and round
And dump
It
In
His
Lap!

(Oh you look so funny, Pillsbury)
And now you're laughing at me
Laughing at me
Laughing! At! Me!

(and not in a mean way or a nasty way no you're laughing like a nice baker boy can you be nice will you be nice?)

The wheels on the bus go round and round,
Syrup!
In!
Your!
Hair!
Round and round.
The wheels on the syrup go round and round
And I
Like
Pillsbury!

Here comes the waitress
Round and round
Here comes the waitress

I don't care and
And
It's boring out here. It's boring in the restaurant Boring here.

Shiro wants out
Oooh, Shiro is angry!

(s'okay, sweet sister, you can come out, I'm done for now)
Done for now.
Done for now.

Shiro can come out round and round Alllll daaaaaay loooooong

(Good-bye! Good-bye, baker boy! Good-bye syrup! Good-bye, salt shaker! Good-bye! Good-bye!)

Chapter Thirty-two

"I certainly hope you are satisfied," I said, leaning back and crossing my arms across my chest.

"Satisfied," Patrick said, rubbing syrup out of his eyes, "is one way to put it."

To my astonishment, he was smiling. I could think of no reason why. The stench of maple by-products was nearly eye-watering, half the restaurant was staring at us, and he was dabbing at his expensive suit with his napkin and mine. It was—I again tried not stare, and again failed.

"Well," Patrick continued. Dab, dab. Smear. Blink. Rub, rub. "Your sister is certainly, uh, energetic."

"You're lucky to be alive, you stupid man." One of the things I so disliked about Adrienne was her sheer unpredictability. She might kill, maim, or smear with syrup. Or all three. Or none of the three.

There was never any way to tell. Absolutely maddening, for

Cadence as well as me. A creature guided entirely by passion, never logic. Revolting. "Do you require first aid?"

"No. Just a dry cleaner."

I was equal parts disgusted, amazed, and relieved. He thought this was funny. Adrienne assaulting him with condiments was *funny*.

I tried to steady my breathing

(don't think about the geese Daddy look out for the geese)

and realized I was clenching both fists. Consciously relaxing, I glanced at the eight pink half-moons I'd gouged into my palms. (Or had that been Cadence?) "I trust you have learned your lesson."

"Oh, sure. You bet. Let's have dinner."

Shocked, I forgot all about my palms as I snapped my head up. *"What?"*

"Is that a request for more information, or—"

"You cannot be serious."

"Sure I am. Anywhere you want to go."

"Have you learned nothing in the past fifteen minutes?"

"Sure I have. Pick you up at eight?"

"Which one of us?" I could actually feel my blood pressure climb. My eyes were all but bugging out of my head.

"Any of you, of course. All of you. You know why I'm still single at the ripe old age of thirty-four? Ice cream."

"Ice cream," I repeated robotically.

"Sure. That's why Baskin-Robbins has thirty-one flavors. I don't *want* vanilla or daiquiri ice or peach or rocky road all the time." He grinned and knuckled away a tear of syrup. "You just might be the perfect girl—girls—for me. So, eight o'clock?"

Ugh. Socializing. Patrick was not in danger—except from his own stupidity—and neither was I. I had overstayed my welcome. Thus it was something of a relief to get the hell out of—

Chapter Thirty-three

"Good gosh! What happened to your suit?"

Patrick was—oh, yech! He was a disaster! (Who smelled terrific; suddenly I was craving French toast in the worst way.) His dark hair was shiny with syrup. His lapels shone stickily. He smelled like a sugaring party. He was smiling at me.

Smiling!

"Ah. You're back. Shiro seemed a little uptight. She didn't stay long. Was it something I said?"

"Oh God." I covered my eyes. "You saw Shiro? Sorry. She's not very sociable. I—"

"She's a little tense," he agreed, "but then, she's got a lot to be tense about. Also, Adrienne felt my suit was missing that syrup touch that means so much."

My hands went numb to the wrist (I evince stress in odd ways); then they fell into my lap, and I realized there were eight little nail marks imprinted on my palms. *Her* bad habit that *I* had to pay for.

I just about shrieked. Oh my God! I'd left the table and

Adrienne had shown up? And thrown a pitcher of syrup on him? And—well, okay, to be fair, that wasn't as bad as it could have been. But still. *So* embarrassing. I was pretty sure Patrick's first visit to Minneapolis was also going to be his last.

"You—you saw all of us?"

"If 'all' means three, then yeppers."

I glanced at my watch. I'd been gone for just under five minutes. We were still in the booth. Adrienne hadn't done any real damage. Neither had Shiro.

Outside of therapy sessions, and the occasional late night with Cathie, I couldn't remember a time when someone had dealt with the three of us in fewer than five minutes. Certainly not a layman, like the baker.

I had no idea what to say to Patrick.

Fortunately, I didn't have to. He did the talking. And before I knew it, I had a date for later.

Which made me wonder: which of us, exactly, was clinically insane?

Chapter Thirty-four

By the time Patrick picked me up (in a different suit, this time with no tie and a bit of chest hair peeking out), I came to a conclusion: I was the insane one. Or more insane, anyway. Why did I think this date was going to work? Jeepers, who puts a guy in danger and then exposes him again less than twenty-four hours later?

It didn't matter whether the guy liked Baskin-Robbins or not. I wasn't an ice-cream chain (though Adrienne, I strongly suspected after waking up one morning with my butt covered in melted mint chocolate chip, frequented them). I was a trained federal agent who could barely restrain herself from causing severe personal injury!

"Date's off," I told him, slamming the door in his face.

He stuck his foot out in time—nice shoes!—and jammed the door open. "Which one of the three of you has cold feet?"

"It doesn't matter. You probably shouldn't force yourself into the house; the next sister who shows up will probably go beyond syrup in wrecking your ass. And you've already had one suit ruined."

"Okay, I'll stay out here in my super-duper SUV. But I'm going to be honking the entire evening."

My eyes narrowed. "You wouldn't."

"Why not? It'll make a fantastic noise throughout the neighborhood, which'll embarrass Cadence. Shiro will be freshly annoyed and agree to anything to make it stop. And yet, none of the three of you will be in any real danger . . . so I don't think I'll be seeing Adrienne at all. See you in the car." And with that, he closed the door on me.

On me!

"Darn it all to hippy-skip!" I checked myself in the foyer mirror. I had gotten dressed and fixed my hair before resolving to end the date, so the blond-locks-on-straps-of-short-black-dress thing was already working for me. But I had no makeup on.

The horn started blaring. It was a fierce tenor

Three Tenors

that made me jump and grit my teeth.

MENH. MENH. MENH. MENNNNNNNNH.

"Okay, I'm—"

MENH-MENH-MENNH. MENNNNH. MENH. MENH.

"I'm—"

MEAAAAANNNNNNNNNNNNNNNNNH.

I whipped the door open and screamed, "Holy buckets on a Popsicle stick, will you let me get a makeup bag and my shoes!?"

He leaned and grinned through the passenger-side window. His hands stayed on the wheel.

MENH.

Within thirty seconds, I was barefoot in the passenger seat, slipping my feet into strappy black heels while trying not to drop the finger-poppin' makeup bag.

"You'd better have a vanity mirror in this chariot, fella."

He flipped the visor down and another flap up. "With lights. We've got plenty of time before we—"

I slapped him. Not too hard.

Surprised, he bit his lip. "Okay. Sorry. Honking was obnoxious."

"Buster, let me share a lesson in dating with you: you don't rush a girl. Ever. When she's doing her best to look good, you just let her work. You're serious about this date?"

"Very serious."

"Take your eyes off my chest and say that again."

He did.

"Well then, you shouldn't have nearly ruined everything by being an ashtray about it."

"But you said you didn't even want to—"

"Have you ever dated? Like, anyone?"

He gestured to the suit and the car. *What do you think?*

"Fine. Somewhere along the way, you must have met a girl who said something she didn't mean."

"One or two."

"Well, now you've met three. At once. Drive, monkey-flapper."

He turned the key in the ignition, paused, and turned to me. "So you've never sworn even once . . . ?"

I didn't look away from the mirror as I flipped open my compact. "Not once. But, buster, you keep talking and I'll bet I get there."

Chapter Thirty-five

Located along Grand Avenue in St. Paul, Ottavio's was the sort of mysterious upscale place I'd drive past on my way to worse neighborhoods (not very far away, to be sure) when solving a crime. It was a refurbished mansion with a hand-painted black-and-gold sign. When Patrick turned into the tiny parking lot, I forgave him a little bit.

"You been here before?" he asked.

"Yeah, don't ya know, all us federal-agent girls like to hang out here after work. Get drunk like fish and score with the men."

"I thought Shiro was the sarcastic one."

"Shiro didn't have to apply her own makeup in a moving vehicle on Interstate 94."

"Hey, okay." The ignition turned off, and he put both hands on me. Fortunately for him, he chose my shoulders. "I am really sorry. If you want me to take you home and leave you alone, I'll do that right now. But I hope you'll tell me you'd still like to have dinner with me. I really want you to have a good time to-night."

My eyes rolled up and took in the moonroof. "Well. I'd hate to cancel a reservation here. Good restaurants can be hard to come by in the Twin Cities. I hear this one's struggling with the recession and all, and it could probably use the business."

He bit the inside of his cheek as he grinned. "For poor Ottavio's sake, then."

"For Ottavio."

Dinner was delightful. I learned how to pronounce "gnocchi" and discovered that "Super Tuscans" were not a group of Italian crime-fighting crusaders with genetically modified powers. I also picked up a few baking tips from my date, made him laugh a few times with my tales of Cathie and me at MIMH, and felt his foot slide up my calf more than once.

When I felt it without a shoe, I knew we had to talk.

"So anyhow," I told him as I reached under, grabbed his sock, yanked it off his startled foot, and threw it across the table at him, "I'm a virgin."

"That's a hell of a pickup line. Can I have my foot back?"

I let go. "I'm not trying to pick you up. I'm trying to finish my crème brûlée. After we're done, you're going to pick up the check and drive me home. I'm going to repay you with a chaste kiss on the cheek. And you're going to drive home and take a cold shower."

"I really blew it with the honking, didn't I?"

"Not at all. That was always your best scenario. I'm saving myself for true love."

"What if you've found it?"

"You mean, what if it's found me and can't wait longer than twenty-four hours? Then it's probably a reckless, thoughtless, horn-honking asteroid that ought to go flip itself over."

"For someone who doesn't ever swear, you sure have a suspiciously ready supply of insults."

"Put your sock back on and ask for the bill."

"As the lady commands."

Don't judge me! I'm a girl with high standards in a man. Besides, this isn't why I'm telling you this part of the story.

On the way out of the restaurant, we noticed three husky teenagers prowling the parking lot. They were huddled near a Cadillac about three spaces away from Patrick's SUV. One of them hid something shiny when they saw us.

My plan was to get in the car quietly and drive off, but Patrick . . . darn it all . . .

"You boys drop something in the parking lot?"

The largest one bit his lower lip and tilted his head. "No, man. In fact we just got here. Got a reservation and everything."

"Enjoy your dinner," I said hurriedly, and then to Patrick: "Let's go."

"Because it looks to me like you're trying to break into that car."

This was true, but I didn't see how antagonizing them was going to stop them. In fact, the one with the shiny metal object—skinnier than the first but with a crazy-looking dirty blond mullet—raised it like a weapon. Why, in fact, it *was* a weapon: a crowbar. *Super.*

"You the police, big man?"

"What if I am?"

"Then you better call for backup," the largest one said. "And while you wait, we may show your girlfriend a good time."

"You should know that she's a virgin—"

"Patrick!"

He grinned at me. Clearly he wasn't worried. He hadn't seen much of my sisters, to be sure—but was he being intentionally provocative?

I had very little time to think about that. Mullet with Crowbar was rounding the SUV's hood and coming at Patrick, and the other two were headed for me, trapping me on the passenger side between the SUV and the next car. Somebody would have to do some—

Chapter Thirty-six

—thing NOW.

A spinning back roundhouse kick is mostly for show in martial arts movies and stuff like *The Matrix*. It often does not work in real life because most criminals we deal with are either trained in martial arts themselves, or are hopped up on so many drugs that a kick like that tickles. For those it does work on—aka the nerds—a simple punch will do.

But to escape two opponents coming from either side, slide over the hood of an SUV, and launch yourself at a tall guy coming at your date with a crowbar—*that* is a good time for a spinning back roundhouse kick.

He spit blood as he fell, spraying it all over the businessman's suit. (Served Mr. Provocative right.) The crowbar clattered to the pavement. I motioned to the other two.

"Come pick it up."

The grisly looking one with the mullet took a step back.

"Look, lady, we didn't mean nothin'. You're a virgin. Got it. We'll just go now."

"Actually, I have been in several consecutive committed relationships, and am not a virgin at all." I picked up the crowbar.

They ran. So I let the crowbar drop again.

"Wow, that was—"

"Shut up and get in the car. No, the passenger side. I will take those keys."

As I got into the car, I checked myself reflexively in the rear-view mirror. My dark, straight bob had barely moved out of place. Not that I normally cared about such things, but it was nice to know that this had been an easy fight. Good training, I supposed.

Which did not excuse *his* behavior.

"You manipulated them." I shot the SUV backward before he even got to close his door, startling him into slamming it shut. He was still clawing for the seat belt when I gunned the vehicle forward out of the parking lot and onto Grand Avenue. "You manipulated my sister."

"That's not—"

"You knew she would hide. You knew I would come out. Why did you want me out there?"

When he did not answer, my mood darkened. "Please do not tell me you were switching girls, hoping for action."

"Not action. Just variety. I told you: I like it when things change."

"So you endangered yourself and your date—"

"Looks like we're both fine."

"—to satisfy your impatience and immaturity. You know, I

think I *can* find you a sister who will give you exactly what you are looking for. . . ."

"What do you . . . oh . . . you mean . . ."

I could feel her coming, as if she knew it was her time. She was never very far

Chapter Thirty-seven

awaaaay we go
oh yea I'm driving and it's a good car a fast car
make it go faster
wheels on the bus go round and
make it go faster
wheels go round and round and round and
        HEY here's Pillsbury and he looks a little scared
                Looks a little scared
                        Syrup in your hair!
And the wheels on the bus go round and
                                WHOOPS almost missed the turn
Hey Pillsbury looks good kinda cute kinda scared
        Kinda not scared
                Hmmmmmmmmmmmmmmmm
                ANOTHER TURN WHOOOOOOOO
That's it. I want him.
        (He definitely. Wants. Me.)
Put your hand there, Pillsbury

Don't

Be

Scared!

We're getting on the highway and the wheels go round

Wheels go round

(Up and down, that's right)

And the cars whoosh by, or is that us?

Oh stop yelling, Pillsbury, we didn't even hit that truck and besides, you were doing so good before you took your hand away

Put

It

Back

I said

Put

It

Back!

PUT YOUR HAND BACK BETWEEN MY LEGS, YOU FUCKING MAN

The wheels go

SCREEEEEEEEEEEEEEEEEEEECH

We're stopped. Why

Did we stop?

WHOOSH the cars go past on the left,

On the right.

Honk honk!

Honk back!

HONK HONK!

This is boring. He's just shouting at me. If he won't fuck me, and my sister likes him so much

She
Can
Have
Him

Chapter Thirty-eight

"Are you nuts?"

I shook my head, trying to figure out where I—

WhaaaaaAAAAAAAAAAaaaaaah

"Cripes, we're in the middle of the highway!"

"No shit! Drive!"

I gunned the engine. The SUV leapt forward.

The vehicle didn't do less than sixty the entire way home, counting side roads. I was scared, and bewildered, and furious, and worst of all the hem of my dress was around my waist and the front of my underwear had been pulled aside. No doubt courtesy of my sister . . . and Patrick!

"Did you get all the action you wanted?" I hissed, screeching to a halt in front of my place.

"Cadence, I—"

"Don't even answer. What even happened to those guys in the parking lot? Did my sister kill them and then jump your bones? Is that what you were after—an exciting time with the freak show? Is that all I am to you?"

"Of course not—"

"I said *don't answer.*" Tears were threatening my cheeks, and I wiped my nose with the hem of my dress—what the frick, it was up far enough anyway. "It's not fair. They think I'm weak. You think I'm weak. So I do all the investigation and all the paperwork and when it comes time to do something fun like break a nose or impress some guy, my sisters get to come out and then they go too far and by the time I'm back, I'm in my boss's office or stopped dead in the middle of frayber-hoppin' Interstate 94. Then I have to solve everything again. *It's not fair!*"

I leapt over the gearshift and landed on his crotch. He groaned, and I reached down to press him with my fist. My other hand clawed at his neck as I kissed him roughly on the mouth. Before he had a chance to enjoy any of it, I took my fist off his crotch, reared back, and slugged him across the jaw.

Wow! He's unconscious!

I was heaving with adrenaline, biting my tongue with unfulfilled desire . . . and quite impressed with how much swing radius the passenger compartment of a Lexus SUV afforded an assailant straddling her adversary.

So *that's* what it feels like! No wonder my sisters keep this all to themselves!

Goose bumps rising, I opened the passenger door, made sure the ignition key was safely in his pocket, locked the doors, and closed him inside. Then I walked up the path to my door, wondering if that vibrator Adrienne had left was still anywhere around inside.

Chapter Thirty-nine

The next morning, I woke up and looked out the bedroom window. Patrick and the SUV had left (presumably together), so my mind turned right away to work. I had one assignment, and I didn't even need to go into the office to carry it out.

Tracy Carr, our precious surviving victim of the ThreeFer Killer, was propped up in her bed at St. Olaf's Metropolitan Hospital, the sheets and blankets pulled all the way to her chin. She was clutching the bedclothes so tightly that all her knuckles were white. All the shades were drawn, but every light was blazing. Yerrgh, fluorescent light. Why not just set a crow free to gouge out your eyeballs? It'll feel the same, and have the same end effect.

"Well, hi there!"

"Hi, Agent Jones."

"You mind . . . ?" I gestured to the empty chair on the left side of the bed.

"No," she said, which I figured was a rather large lie. It was a phenomenon I'd seen before. Female victims, no matter how upset or scared or nervous or tired, inevitably chose courtesy over their own wants, even their own needs. She didn't want me to sit down. She didn't want me to be in the same building.

And who could blame her? *I* didn't want to be in the same building, either. If Shiro had been there, she'd have yaked ad nauseam about the weakness of the modern woman, yak-yak, and if Adrienne

(please God not again anytime soon, cut me some slack, okay, God?)

but I just felt sorry for someone who'd let herself be unhappy to avoid the appearance of rudeness.

"I hear they're kicking you loose after lunch."

She nodded. They'd kept her overnight for observation, standard op per St. Olaf's Hospital. I was to try another interrogation, go away, come back to drive her to the safe house on Lake Street, try to get even more info, then go away and discover a clue and solve the case. Sure. And after that I'd find a cure for AIDS, flip the switch in the ancient temple that kept men thinking like pigs, and clean out my fridge.

And I'd have to do all that while keeping things nice and casual, like we were discussing the last movie we'd seen as opposed to, you know, the whole "congrats on escaping the clutches of a madman, now tell me everything no matter how embarrassing or personal" thing.

"D'you want something? A pop? Crackers? Another pillow?" An anti-amnesia machine? The ability to reverse time? Washable cashmere?

Tracy shook her head. Her eyes were so big I could see the

whites all the way around her pupils. She looked like a horse getting ready to flee the glue factory.

"Listen," I said, sitting down. My fingers felt sticky and I peered at them, puzzled—then realized I still had a bit of maple syrup on the first two fingers on both hands. Damn it! I thought I'd washed it all off, but the stuff never leaves your skin.

I sat on my fingers and gave her my brightest nothing-wrong-here smile. All praise to the wanting-to-please stage of assault, because she was sitting there pretending there was nothing wrong with a klutzy federal agent who smelled like syrup. Poor Tracy Carr! "So, I wanted to talk about yesterday some more."

"I assumed you were here to trade recipes for fudge." She deadpanned the comment, but it perked me up all the same. She shows some spunk! Less than twenty-four hours after an ordeal which would leave most people gibbering and drooling in a rubber room! Excellent. If I weren't sitting on my sticky hands, I'd be applauding.

"Fudge, huh? Maybe later. Anyway, the best way for us to lock him—it's a him, right?—in a tiny windowless concrete block for the next four decades—a block without cable or TiVo, I might add—with awful, awful food—and really *terrible* ambience—"

This earned me a tiny smile, more like an involuntary twitch of the lips.

"—well, then we need to talk about yesterday some more." I leveled my best serious look at her, not unlike the look I'd leveled at Patrick the previous night after his honkfest.

"Okay."

Chapter Forty

So we ran through the deep dark details again, starting with the easy stuff. Poor victims! They had to tell the same story to at least twenty different people. Unfortunately, we currently didn't have a better way to do it at that time.

Her name, Tracy Carr. Address: she was renting a furnished hotel room at the Pyrenees in Bloomington, pending the sale of her house back in North Dakota—she'd been in the Twin Cities for nine months. This was common; as lovely as North Dakota was, lots of residents came southeast for job opportunities, late-night social life, or even just a bit more excitement.

She certainly found that last one, I thought ruefully.

She had turned thirty-three in March ("Now I have lived as long as Christ," which, sadly, was not the weirdest thing a survivor ever said to me); she had been born in, of all places, Ankara, Turkey, of an American mother; she had dual citizenship. Her English was precise, almost clipped. She had never known her father. Her mother died when she was a teenager.

My pen flew as I took notes, my writing so horrible that only Shiro and Michaela could have read it. Speed before accuracy! Wait. That was entirely incorrect. Never mind.

Tracy was a freelance accountant who worked from her hotel room. Not a big family; she had two siblings but didn't have much interest in contacting them. (One was not too far away in South Dakota, but the other was in the Southwest—"maybe Arizona," she said wistfully. Given our winters up here, I couldn't blame her.) No, she didn't want me to call anyone for her—the doctors and nurses had already asked. No cousins, aunts, grandparents, pets, dependents, library cards.

She shopped for food occasionally (I made a mental note to have people check out the places she spent money most often; memo to me: pull her credit card receipts) but mostly ordered takeout.

No, she had never seen him before. In fact, in her rush to get out of the dining room, she'd gotten little more than a glance at him: tall, very tall. Slope-shouldered. "Like a farmer," she added. "If he'd been wearing overalls, he would have looked exactly like that—like someone who worked the earth. But he had on jeans and a denim shirt. Short-sleeved."

Lank hair the color of mud; no idea of the eye color. Oh, swell. With such a precise and detailed description, we'd probably have him locked up by lunchtime.

She had called 911 on her cell, from the pantry, while listening to the screams. And the murders.

"Good thing you had it charged," I commented. Memo to me: pull all of her phone records. Whom she called, what they said—the works. And get a transcript of the 911 call if George didn't have it sitting on my desk already.

"Yes."

Chances were a few other agents were doing all these tasks and more, but I'd be wise to follow up. Clues often came from even the most obvious sources, no matter how often the bad guy watched *Law & Order, CSI,* and *The Martha Stewart Show.*

Something was niggling at the base of my spinal cord, and the more I tried to ignore it, the more weirded out I got. It was Tracy. Something about her—her—what? Speech? Facial expressions?

No, it went deeper than that. Something beyond being a victim, even. Something sad, something that had lasted a long time, maybe even something from her youth. I didn't know what to do with that; but I'd been doing this job too long to blow off any hunch, no matter how unlikely or unpleasant or just plain silly.

"No," she replied to my last question, which, fortunately, I hadn't yet forgotten. Not a muscle moved except those controlling her mouth. "I never go to a gym. It's too hard."

"Yeah, I have trouble finding time to work out, too," I replied, only half listening. It was a partial truth—Shiro got more than enough exercise for all three of us—and I was still distracted.

Tracy had just given me a big clue and she didn't realize what it was. Neither did I. What was it about? "Plus," I continued, not having any idea what was going to come out of my mouth next, "I hate getting my sweat all over the treadmill. Who wants to mop up her own sweat? Never mind anyone else's. Makes me feel like I'm trapped in the hold of a ship."

"And it's hard," Tracy added.

Jeepers, what was it? And was it even important? It must

be or it wouldn't be bugging me so much. Something I knew. Something I hadn't known last night that I knew now, if I could just—

I whirled and glared at a passing nurse. "Will you please change out her IV bag before the fu—I mean, the freaking thing reverses itself?"

Startled, the nurse paused in midstep. Tracy's eyes were big. "Pardon?"

"Da . . . darn it all!"

"Pardon?"

"Uh—just remembering I forgot to pick up my dry cleaning." There was no hope for it. I'd have to ask Shiro. Good Lord, I was letting anybody drive my body these days.

God knew when she'd let me come back.

Too bad. Shiro would know. She would come straight out and say

Chapter Forty-one

"You suffer from Asperger's syndrome."

The live victim blinked at me. Her knuckles were still white, but she had lowered the bedclothes to her waist, revealing a clean dark blue scrubs top. She smelled like clean cotton and tape—tape everywhere. Holding the IV needle in place; closing the small cut over her left eyelid; tape at the crook of her elbow where they had drawn for labs. The smell of anger. The smell of fear.

"What?"

"Asperger's. It is difficult for you to go to the gym because of all the faces."

"Oh yes!" Tracy Carr didn't nod, but her eyes crinkled in acknowledgment of a sort. "The faces."

"And you cannot read expressions."

"No."

"You never know if someone is mad or sad or just having a bad day." I studied Tracy Carr. Her expression during what would be—for most people—an odd, distressing, anxiety-inducing, uncomfortable conversation had not flickered in the slightest. Cadence would have gotten it eventually. She was simply too invested in putting the victim at ease. Which occasionally had its place during an interrogation.

I had other concerns.

After another long pause, I said, "It is like a language, right? A code most people know but you don't. It is . . . maddening. Right?"

Tracy nodded so hard I was afraid she would strike her head on the table-on-wheels which held her supper and the button. "Yes, that's right. It's as if I skipped a workshop that everyone else in the world attended at least twice."

"I have had that impression myself," I muttered, and to my surprise, Tracy smiled. I never made anyone smile. Not on purpose.

What Cadence had assumed was shock the night before was really the typical affect of Asperger's. Occasionally people assumed it was a disability I suffered from myself. Which just goes to show how stupid some people were. Also, there was this damned obsessive need to categorize everything. Are you white, are you a smoker, what is your median income? Do you like classical music, are you allergic to dairy, are you a Democrat?

I could hardly get up on a high horse of morals about such behavior, though. Had I not been in a rush to figure out what was wrong with Tracy Carr, so I could file her neatly away in my brain and go into hiding until the twit wearing my body needed me again?

Tracy Carr certainly had several of the classic signs. She had tripped against Cadence last night as she walked with her to the ambulance. She said things inappropriate to the situation because she was trying to figure out how she was *supposed* to feel, and then imitating that.

And she had that peculiar affect so indicative of Asperger's; she had no natural ability to read facial expressions. She would have to have been taught that *this* is a smile and it means you are happy; *this* is a frown and it means you are not.

"Did you get diagnosed in Turkey?"

She laughed bitterly and shook her head. "No, it was years later. In the States. My parents . . . well." She shrugged.

"Do you indulge in obsessive rituals? I realize that is private, but we would ask anything to catch the ThreeFer."

She smiled at me again as if we had a great and wonderful secret. "I count toothpicks. Even if it's a new box and it *says* how many on the box and I *know* fourteen have been used and I know I counted them yesterday, I always have to count them again. And again. I count napkins, too." She paused. "And paper clips. Oh, and binder clips. And forks. And—"

I cut her off with an impatient gesture. Yes, yes, this was sounding right. Although it was closely related to autism, those with Asperger's did not completely withdraw from society. And they tended to be brilliant. But they would be awkward at a party, a wedding, a bar. They took more comfort in books than in socialization.

Hmm. Perhaps I *did* have Asperger's.

Well. An issue for another time.

Chapter Forty-two

"Asperger's!" I cried, starting to stand—and then I realized I already was. I hate when she just wanders around in my body like that. You would not *believe* the places I've found myself.

Don't ask, though. I'll never, never tell.

Tracy Carr blinked at me with wide, watery eyes. *Easy, Cadence. Let's not startle her into a coma, or a head cold.* "Yes, we established that."

"Right, right." I knew Shiro would figure it out. But the ThreeFer, still lurking out there, wouldn't wait for my poor drowning brain to figure these things out. Also, it just kept *bugging* me. "I was just, um, testing you. Okay, you ready to leave?"

She was, yanking so hard she pulled me off of my feet. I stumbled and nearly knocked over the IV stand. Cadence Jones, ladies 'n' gents, making another graceful exit. Oooh, yergh, watch out for the bedpans.

The admitting doc, a harassed-looking woman in her early

thirties with the *weirdest*-colored eyebrows I had ever seen (blue!), made Tracy sign paperwork, made her pee (what was it with the medical profession's obsession with the function of removal?), and then insisted on wheeling her to the front door, where I'd parked. Just a few more steps and we'd be in my reasonably priced Mitsubishi Eclipse.

Now, don't jump to any conclusions. I wasn't stealing a parking spot from the handicapped; it's just that as a federal agent I had certain privileges. If a blind person drove up, of course I would have given her the parking space. Jeepers, I wasn't a *monster.*

Never mind! I had sprung Tracy from the hospital, like the Rita Hayworth poster had sprung Andy Dufresne from Shawshank Prison, and now work awaited us. Well, me. Onward!

I took a deep breath and sighed. It was one of those Minnesota autumn days when the wind was gentle and the trees were towering red and yellow and orange giants. When the sky was dotted with little clouds that looked like popcorn, and the sun was warm on my back. When I was hot on the trail of a repeat offender, and Starbucks served pumpkin-flavored coffee.

Ah! Fall. I loved fall. It was—

Chapter Forty-three

"I hate fall."

Tracy Carr glanced at me while she fumbled for a cigarette, dropping her purse on the pavement and looking as though she might burst into tears at any second. Good Lord, I hoped she would not cry. The very sound set my teeth on edge.

I picked up her purse and watched as she dug out a lighter. I looked at this insanity with irritation. "There must be a cancer pill you can just take and get it over with, correct?"

"What? I—what?"

"There are much, much quicker ways—efficient ways, cost-effective ways—to commit suicide." Hypocritical? No. *I* only had a pack a year. Few smokers possessed my self-control.

"Suicide? I would never—suicide?"

Chapter Forty-four

"—love fall!" I had to yank on the wheel to avoid plowing into a speed-limit sign—Shiro had left me in mid-drive, which I supposed was better than how Adrienne had left me the night before. "It's not too hot, but also it's too cold for the bugs, and all the kids are running around with their new backpacks. And the gorgeous leaves—what the heck is that?"

Tracy twisted so far away from me she was practically hanging on to the wipers. "What? The geese? They're just migrating."

"Oh. Sure. I wasn't—"

(Daddy look out look out look out!)

"—scared or anything. No." I swallowed. "I wasn't scared at all. I was startled for a second. That's all. Listen." I shifted and merged onto 35W. "We can't force you to stay in a safe house—I have to say, Tracy, that shows bad judgment, and I'm sorry to have to tell you such a mean thing. But since you've (foolishly) refused, we'll have at least two agents on you at all times."

"He won't come after me again." Tracy sounded tired, but sure of herself. "I'm old news to him. I don't exist anymore to him. He thinks it's art. He thinks I'm art."

"What?"

"ART," she said, so loudly I flinched away. Yep, time for a visit to my friendly neighborhood ear, nose, and throat guy. "I said he thinks he's making art. There's nothing for me to be afraid of anymore. It's like a painter worrying the canvas will come after him; hardly worth thinking about, much less fretting. He *made* me, he made the other two gentlemen. I'm just a thing to him now. It isn't in his head that we're real people with emotions and needs. Who cares what a sculpture thinks, anyway?"

"Very profound." I pondered that, merging smoothly—hardly any traffic this late in the morning. Tracy was just right. Exactly right. Odd that a civilian could pick up on that so quickly—and express it so well. Poor thing.

We were at the hotel in no time, and I walked Tracy inside, clearing the room, making sure there wasn't a bogeyman hiding under the bed, and confiscating her complimentary sewing kit. She likely couldn't hurt herself with a needle, a black button, and a thimble (unless she swallowed it, maybe), but I was taking no chances.

The place was neat and clean, and decorated in modern inoffensive. A coffee table, a small couch, a stuffed chair with a teeny stuffed pillow. Dining area just off the living room—a simple blond oak table with three chairs. A double bed sporting a truly hideous jack-o'-lantern–orange fringed(!) bed-spread.

No pictures, just a print of a girl in toe shoes up *en pointe,* looking graceful as all get-out. I love that. It's—

Chapter Forty-five

"That is the tackiest thing I have ever seen. Toe shoes? Pink toe shoes? Show us the blisters, you nameless foot model. Show us the calluses."

Chapter Forty-six

"—it's just so classy and delicate—ow!" I barked my knee on the coffee table—how'd I get all the way over here?

"Hey! Tracy Carr! Little help?"

Tracy Carr, however, just stood in the middle of the room and clearly had no idea what to do with her hands.

"Well, this is—um—homely. Homey! I meant homey." Like any one of a dozen in the neighborhood, it was basically a beehive for people. The walls were neutral cream; the carpet was a dark gray that hid dirt. There was a tiny kitchen with an even tinier stove; the plant on the counter was a fake.

It was the kind of place where middle management stayed while they were waiting for a new office, or traveling salesmen. Heck, we were an airline hub—the whole street was practically flight attendant alley. At least they hadn't started charging by the hour.

It was best not to talk about the wallpaper. You'll thank me later. Believe me.

"Thank you for bringing me back. I'll come to the government building tomorrow to do more paperwork."

"That'd be swell." I pointed at the only photograph in the room, a four-by-six of three teenagers standing around a big white house that badly needed a paint job, shingles, and a screen door. "Is that your family when you were all little?" There was something about the house. It didn't just stand around them, it *loomed* over them. And all three faces were pale and pinched, like they had a vitamin deficiency.

Tracy nodded.

"Well, that looks—" I tried to think of something nice to say. In reality, I felt as far away from Tracy Carr as whatever sibling was in Arizona, or Nevada, or wherever in the Southwest. Maybe they felt that way about her, too, no matter where they lived. Maybe in this very picture, they were already splitting apart from the weird sister with the "funny syndrome." It probably made them more popular with their peers to distance themselves, and children can be cruel.

Well, in any case, how on earth was I going to help all of that now? I'd helped debrief her, overseen her hospital release, and made small talk. Also, I had offered to swing by McDonald's for some Filets-O-Fish, which she'd declined. So now I could get a move on. And not a moment too soon. There were probably reams of paperwork for me to thrash through back at the office.

A live victim, hooray, at last, praise Jesus; I knew this was a big step in getting close to ThreeFer. More work, yep. And that was just fine.

Chapter Forty-seven

Sure enough, there was, scattered menacingly over my mouse pad, covering my chair, and burying my Little Mermaid desk blotter. Plenty of data, but not much analysis. That would come; it always did—I just hoped it wouldn't be too late. You know what they say about hindsight and twenty-twenty vision and a step in time saves nine and birds and bushes and such.

And the thing of it was, we probably already had the killer's name. Somewhere in all those piles of police reports, federal paperwork, witness write-ups (although there'd been precious little of those this time around), lab services, background checks, CODIS (ha! not much biological evidence this time, either), FOIPA file dumps (or, as George put it, "Hippie Law 101"—he was virulently and unreasonably opposed to the Freedom of Information Act), even DVDs of the crime scenes and files with a thousand little facts . . . somewhere in all that junk was one little thing that would tie all these victims together. Some one dumb thing that would seem so obvious to us after the fact.

Only after the fact.

The process was mind-boggling and seemed insurmountable, like the *People* magazine crossword puzzle after you'd been on a desert island long enough to miss a season of *American Idol,* but that was no reason to take shortcuts. And I couldn't go back on the street in good conscience until I'd taken a crack at it.

It was like . . . ahmmm . . . how can I put this? It was like making yourself eat the baked potato before you could have the hot fudge sundae. When you were allergic to baked potatoes. And it hadn't been washed before being wrapped in foil and plunked in the oven. And the oven would only heat up to room temperature.

As far as Shiro and I were concerned, it was simple discipline. I knew enough about myself (hurrah for years of psychotherapy) to understand I was *so* easily distracted; not so with Shiro the laser beam. And what was a simple disciplinary action for one sister was bamboo under the fingernails for Adrienne, who couldn't analyze data unless she set it on fire first.

And speaking of analysis, that was enough of it for now. Enough stalling while pretending I wasn't stalling. Time to get to work! Uh, analyzing. I scooped up about a thousand manila folders and stacked them (semi)neatly on the corner of my desk. I had now exposed a whopping nine by fourteen inches of bare space. Which I promptly filled with NNCP paperwork.

Cathie once walked into my bedroom and saw a small spot of exposed rug that was not covered in dirty clothes, clean clothes, magazines, books, bananas, strawberry body butter, teacups, *The Tudors* DVDs, a curling iron, pot holders, or CDs. Her prompt reaction was to scream, "Oh my dear God, there's *floor*!" and then frantically kick my gym clothes and soft billowy granny underpants onto the brazen empty space, filling it while she screeched like a storm siren. I'd laughed so hard I spilled my ginger ale all over myself.

And oh my, look at this. A couple of BOFFO detectives approached, summing me up with their long beaky noses and deep-set blue eyes. There were identical shiny spots on their suits, too, and they were both advertising their premature male pattern baldness by combing their hair sideways across the tops of their heads.

Honestly. Do guys *really* think that will fool us? "Whoa, hi there, John. Gosh, for a second there I thought you were going bald, but I see now that you have a full, lush head of hair. Which grows sideways from left to right in sticky strands. Have I ever been this sexually excited? I think not!"

And here they were, blocking the soothing glow banks of fluorescent lighting with their shiny suits. Just when I assumed my day couldn't get any worse. Why did I always assume that? It was like daring the gods.

Slope-shouldered and unibrowed, Frick and Frack were veteran agents who had been partners so long they actually resembled each other, you know, like pet owners are supposed to resemble their pets. Seriously. George, Tina, and I agreed it was a little frightening. Not least because we weren't sure which one was the pet.

"So," Frick greeted me. "Who y'gonna be after lunch, Jones, that crazy chick or the karate bitch?" This was his idea of a warm, friendly hello, often accompanied by a greedy glance at my breasts via his peripheral vision.

"It's already after lunch, Dennis," I replied pleasantly. "And I'm me."

"Yeah, but how come that wildcat Adrienne was here?" Frack stared at me while he blinked slowly. Like an owl. An aging, potbellied, balding, child-support-payment-dodging, passive-aggressive, Dairy Queen–addicted owl. To ramp up the ickiness factor, they stood in for each other, one asking questions the other one wanted answers for. Like a ventriloquist's dummy. They were interchangeable!

"You'd have to ask her." I felt perfectly safe saying this, because neither Frick nor Frack went near Adrienne if they could help it, the one sensible habit they had acquired over the years. And they'd never risk *asking* for her. "You know, the next time you see her."

"So how come you're catching fer ThreeFer?" I had been watching carefully, hoping I would finally be able to categorize them as separate entities. The one on the left had spoken this time. Yikes. I had met serial rapists who were more pleasant. "Cuz we thought you had that thing." He turned to his partner. "You know. The thing."

"The thing in Duluth," Frick corrected.

Ah. Duluth. The "thing" was Internet fraud; you know, that spam e-mail from the mysterious Moroccan government official? Her name was Audrey Swenson, she was born in Superior, Wisconsin, she couldn't *spell* Morocco much less be a national, and I'd made a vow to see her in a cell before hockey season started.

But of course, I didn't work only her file; like everyone

here, I juggled a full caseload and, like every government employee, prayed for our budget to keep up with our rent.

And why in the world were Frick and Frack so darned interested in my caseload? Had they lost a bet? Was this the warm-up to (oh please God no no *no*!) asking me out?

"Yeah, so how come?"

Less than fifty-five seconds into the conversation and they'd lost me. Funny how fifty-five seconds could seem like years and years and years. And years. "How come what?"

"How come you're catching fer Threefer?"

"Oh!" Frack was staring down at a TS/SCI memo (boo! bad cube etiquette!), upon which I casually dropped a copy of the invitation to Tina's housewarming. "Gee, I thought you knew."

"If we knew, we wunt be askin'."

"You wunt? All righty. Well, you see, we fearless government minions of the FBI have this pesky thing called 'federal jurisdiction.' And that means when there's a crime like kidnapping or murder or counterfeiting or election fraud or oil spills or insurance fraud or art theft or gem theft, we are pledged to examine the clues and catch the bad guys, as is our sworn duty mandated by the attorney general of the United States and also mentioned in our union contract. These actions, which fall within our 'jurisdiction,' are known commonly as 'fighting crime' or 'earning a living,' during which—"

"Yeah, you're as funny as a crotch."

I rolled my eyes and sighed. "Crutch. Funny as a crutch." You had to have at least a four-year college degree to join our illustrious ranks; I occasionally wondered how Frick and Frack had managed to fake the necessary paperwork. Surely the University of Nebraska hadn't *really* released these two into the wild. "Well, gee whiz, fellas. This has been just superfun. But I have to—" Wash my hair. Go bowling. Clean my shotgun. Return the new Dolly Parton tell-all to Barnes and Noble. Hang myself. "—uh—I have to—"

"Cuz y'know, we c'n help you with it."

It took every shred of concentrated effort, every drop of willpower I had ever possessed, to keep the horror-struck expression off my face. "Oh. Well. That is just so nice, fellas. But you—um—that is to say, *I* have to—well—" My sense of self-preservation grimly battled my incessant need to be polite to absolutely everyone, all the time. "It's not that I'm not grateful, or need the help, it's that—"

Michaela stomped down the aisle through our cubes, a kielbasa clutched in one fist, her suit jacket primly buttoned to just below her nipples. "You!" she snapped, green eyes bulging as her blood pressure climbed. "And you! Where are your expense reports, you useless boobs?"

"Heh."

"She said boobs," the other one added. They turned in scary unison—now they were rejects from Michael Flatley's *Lord of the Dance.* They stepped in unison, shiny pant legs flashing in the fluorescents. Now they were *Terminator* bureaucrats—and marched off to wherever the heck it was they needed to go when they weren't torturing me. I was so relieved I actually saw spots for a few seconds.

Chapter Forty-eight

Nope! That was George, my partner. He had changed ties. Again. The spots I had seen were actually a pattern of tiny green mice running through a vermilion field of bright yellow mousetraps. *This meant something!* I was sure of it. Dr. Nessman probably knew all about it.

"What did those two freaks want?" he said, throwing himself into his office chair. He shot past me and nearly collided with the printer, then kicked off the cube wall above it with his tastefully loafered feet. "God, I can't stand those two." He whizzed past me again, this time on the left. Keeping eye contact with George was sometimes akin to watching the ball in one of those old-timey pinball machine things. "Did you *see* their suits?"

"You're, uh, aware of the irony, you calling them freaks and criticizing their clothing choices while at the same time—"

"Off my case, Blue's Clues." His nearly black hair fell into his eyes and he jerked his head back, raking his fingers through his long bangs. His nails gleamed with the latest no-polish manicure. If George ever felt stress about anything, it sure didn't show on his hands.

"I don't know what that means," I admitted, beginning to paw through the paperwork again. I thought about my partner, and about Frick's partner. "George? D'you ever wonder what you'd be doing if BOFFO didn't need us?"

His eyes narrowed and his long nose twitched as if he smelled sour milk. "No."

Of course not. This was Mr. Live for Today, after all. He would never—

"I don't have to wonder," he continued matter-of-factly. "I know. I'd be cooling my heels somewhere on death row, being a sadass jailhouse lawyer and filing my own appeals while locked up twenty-three hours a day and fielding marriage proposals from women I'd never met."

Uh. Hmm. Okay. Also: he was probably right.

"And you'd be locked in a rubber room somewhere, being polite to the orderlies when Shiro wasn't busting heads and Adrienne wasn't eating the stuffing out of the rubber walls."

Also probably right. "Ooookay."

"Come on. It's nothing you don't know. The only good thing about BOFFO needing people like us is that it makes me feel better that I need BOFFO."

I eyed my abrasive unpleasant handsome homicidal partner and tried to keep the expression of surprise off my face. It wasn't like George to show deep understanding—about anything.

"Don't look so baffled, Cadence. Tell me it wasn't the luckiest day of your life when Michaela recruited you right out of the MIMH."

"It was a lucky day," I admitted. It had also been years ago, but it still seemed surreal.

An older woman, serene and powerful, with eyes the color of leaves and running shoes that were blindingly white, waiting for me when I finished my session with the shrink du jour. An older woman showing me federal identification and explaining that there was a branch of the FBI that could use my special skills.

And not a new branch, either. The FBI had been started in 1908 under President Teddy Roosevelt, with a whopping thirty-four agents.

BOFFO had been started in 1910, with four.

We've always been there. To protect, and serve, and go crazy: that was our mission, our pleasure, and, occasionally, our burden. The government always needed people who didn't look at the world the way "norms" did. The government always needed people to use. And use up.

I had, at the time, assumed Michaela was crazier than I was. Which still might be true, if Shiro ever told me why she was so obsessed with cutlery. But Michaela had made a believer out of me. All three of us. And so I'd been serving the public at the pleasure of the federal government, with all the head shrinking I could stand thrown in for free. It was like winning a lottery that rewarded insanity with a high-risk occupation and firearm training.

"I still don't know how Michaela finds us. Found us," George was saying. "I nearly shit myself when she bailed me out of lockup in St. Paul that time. Fast-forward nine months, I'm wearing suits to work and fending off Secret Santa drawings, my partner's a multiple personality, my boss is obsessed with chopping vegetables, and my shrink makes me take the MMPI every nine months."

"Oooh, yuck." The MMPI was a nightmare quiz with hundreds of T/F questions. I could actually feel my will to live draining away whenever I had to sit down to the cursed thing.

"Why the dumb questions, anyway? You thinking about quitting? Being a crazy civilian again, instead of a crazy government employee?"

"Nooooo. I just wonder . . . sometimes . . . what it's all for. And why we keep doing it."

"Yeah, you would." He shrugged. "You think too much."

And you don't think at all, my sociopathic friend.

"Are we going to lunch? We're going. Are we gonna have lunch? Let's have lunch."

"Well, no."

"Then what the hell am I doing here?"

"I haven't the slightest idea in the world."

George chewed on his lips like an angry horse for a few seconds, then glanced back in the direction of Frick and Frack's departure. "So what'd they want?"

"I don't know, but it was a little strange."

He snorted.

"Even for them," I clarified, "or us. They were awfully interested in my caseload."

"Your caseload or our caseload?"

"ThreeFer Killer."

His eyes went narrow and squinty, and I realized anew that he and Michaela both had the purest green eyes I'd ever seen. Not hazel, not brown-gold. Green. *Green* green. It was rare. Also, in another thousand years it would be nonexistent—

everybody'd have the same skin color and eye color. I considered telling George what his descendants would miss out on . . . and then I realized he'd probably never have any. Sociopaths made disastrous spouses and even worse parents. The world—the galaxy—would be a safer place if George never reproduced.

I mentally shook myself like a puppy leaving a pond. "I have some paperwork to go through."

"I care," my insane partner snapped.

I blinked. Even for George, this was a little—oh. Oh! How stupid. How could I have forgotten?

Well. It had been a busy day.

"You look fine," I said as nicely as I could.

His scowl deepened. His forehead was actually laddered with angry frown wrinkles. His eyes gleamed at me like a pissed-off wolf's.

"And that's a—a—a *lovely* tie," I added, trying not to look at the awful thing.

He brightened and stroked it. "You think so?"

"Just, um, gorgeous. Really very absolutely extremely beautiful."

George was thirty today. He found aging quite stressful. His vanity was matched only by his hideous neckties.

"Let me get this junk out of the way and then we can go to Culver's to celebrate."

"Culver's?"

"Frozen custard," I wheedled. "Chocolate. Nuts. Hot fudge sauce. A Mountain Dew with lots of ice. *Two* Mountain Dews."

He brightened. "You promise?"

"Sure! But later. I have to get this done."

"Okay." He jumped up. "Okay! So, later. Okay." He rushed off, to whatever destiny awaited federally employed sociopaths on their birthdays.

I got back to it, realizing I'd been dealing with people for almost an hour as opposed to actually working. As I'm pretty sure I said, trudging through reams of paperwork created a bit of resentment.

I scanned the file as rapidly as I could and still retain the info. I stared at the crime-scene photos, read up (again) on the victims.

The victims. I was sure that was where the common thread was lying around, just waiting for someone (me!) to pick it up. ThreeFer was driven to these particular people.

He'd killed tourists and lifelong residents of the area. He'd killed men and he'd killed women. African Americans and whites. Models and tax attorneys. Waitresses and doctors. The only thing—the *one* thing—they had in common, the thing obvious since the first crime scene, was there were always three of them, set in some sort of odd tableau that stumped us but clearly had deep, deep meaning for the killer. And they were killed the same way.

Killed gently, if such a thing was possible (it was, actually). Stab wounds to the chest—the heart, specifically.

No defensive wounds.

Not so much as a scratch. ThreeFer wasn't drugging them, wasn't getting them drunk. He was soothing them, calming them—and they never fought when the knife slipped in.

Not a single one of them fought. That, more than anything, stuck in my brain, stuck in Shiro's, too. We knew people fought to live. It was both awful and wonderful, the way we clung to life. The damage we could take, would take—to stay alive.

Yes. Awful. And wonderful.

A painting didn't fight; neither did a sculpture. They just let themselves be made.

Could Tracy Carr be right? Was he working on what he thought was his art? Could he stop himself if he wanted? Like my friend Cathie couldn't *not* scrub her kitchen floor with a toothbrush? Or how George could never walk away from his own reflection, physically or metaphorically?

No. ThreeFer couldn't stop. He wouldn't stop. That whole "please catch me before I kill again; I secretly wish to be stopped which is why I left a fingerprint at the last crime scene" is one of the biggest myths in law enforcement.

Because they never wanted to stop. If they wanted to stop, they would. ThreeFer wouldn't, and why? Because making his art made him Leonardo da Vinci, Picasso, and God rolled up into one divinely talented sandwich. He would never, ever give that up.

It made me wonder: what wasn't *I* giving up?

Chapter Forty-nine

After a couple hours of analytic drudgery, I decided I owed Cathie (or did I owe myself?) a quick call. I shoved some folders off my desk, found my cell phone (neatly clipped to my belt—thank goodness they'd started making them small!), and tapped her number.

It rang, and rang, and rang, until it was snatched up and a very groggy voice moaned, "Whoever this is? Mmm. You better be on *fire*. D'you know what time it is?"

"It's me. Cadence." Ever helpful, I added, "Cadence Jones?"

"Cadence, we've been friends for over a decade. I know your frigging last name. Why are you bugging me at the crack of dawn?"

"Because it's the crack of noon. How'd your meeting with the art guy go?"

Another pitiful sound, this time between a groan and a whimper. "Why d'you think I'm so damned hungover?"

I eyeballed a few e-mails—oh man, they were going to try the Secret Santa thing *again*. Why, why, why? Hadn't they learned from last year's debacle? The Secret Santa ritual was the perfect thing to make paranoids more paranoid, the kleptomaniacs steal more, and the social misfits fit worse.

One poor colleague thought I was shooting rays into her brain from my bra straps, to punish her for taking the gift I had specifically bought for her. I went braless for a week (in January! *January!*) but she would never believe I wasn't stealing her thoughts with my C cups. It's better now. She's more comfortable in the lab than she ever was in the field.

"It was great! He was great." Uh-oh. Cathie was still sharing the lewd details of her evening. I'd better pay attention.

Her dates were, apparently, more energetic than mine. Hey, I could date. I *have* dated. So have my sisters. Adrienne, of course, dated too much. But even Shiro had a girlfriend a while ago. Lucy (or was it Lucia?) dumped her the second time Adrienne showed up.

This suggests Shiro's gay, but I think she's more attracted to the person inside. So far, the people inside—Lucy, Betty, Ellen, and Madison—have all been women. According to Cathie, who asked my sister (since I couldn't), she had loved every one of them exclusively, and had her heart broken each time. Because of her sisters, one of whom wasn't gay, and one of whom was *everything*.

Meanwhile, Cathie was still twittering in my ear. "That guy knows his Rembrandts from his van Goghs, if you know what I mean."

"I don't, actually." Tina wandered by and set a Frappuccino on my desk, and I winked at her. I clawed frantically for my purse, dug, and waved another pasta recipe at her for her party this weekend. She nodded, took it, and went on her way.

I decided to rejoin the conversation. Not that I ever had the upper hand when it came to Cathie. "So, I'm glad you had a good evening."

"To put it mildly, fruitcake." Only Cathie could disparage my admittedly ragged neurosis without suffering a loud, agonizing death. "Sorry about missing breakfast yesterday. I haven't talked to Patrick. How'd it go?"

"You haven't seen him today?" It occurred to me she might not even know about the date. A mild panic set in. What if Patrick never came home?

"No. Hang on." I heard her walking down the hall with the portable. "Patrick? He's not in his room. Of course, if it's noon, he's probably wheeling and dealing around town. . . . But I'll check the kitchen."

A few moments later, we had our answer. "He left a note on the counter." She giggled. "It says: 'Don't ask.' "

I couldn't hold back a snort. "You wouldn't have believed it if you'd been there."

"No way!" Right away Cathie sounded more awake. "So dish on the breakfast. Shiro hopped out of you and julienned his ham loaf?"

"Don't I wish. It was Adrienne. She threw syrup on him and he liked her. He liked Shiro, too. He asked us out that night, and we went!"

"Which one?"

"All of us!" I howled, the true horror of the situation finally sinking in. *I ended the date by coldcocking him. Who does that?*

"All right, calm down before you pop a vein."

"You never mind my veins."

"So how'd the date go?"
I told her.
She hung up, laughing.
I was just about to return to work when

Chapter Fifty

I turned my attention to the screen, and the desk full of files around it. Cadence had gotten the investigation off to a good start, but she was clearly overwhelmed emotionally. She needed help, she was feeling resentful, and it was time to pitch in with more than a flying sidekick.

Pam glided by, dressed in her penguin flannel pajamas and carrying several case files. I snapped my fingers to get her attention.

"What, I'm your dog? I'm a trained seal?"

I was unmoved by the girl's irritation. I had a job to do and so did she. And I was really very hungry. Some things could not wait. "Hush. I require copies of this, this, and this. And please arrange a data dump within the next two hours."

"Do I look like I've cloned myself?" She nodded down at the paperwork she was dragging around. "Can't you see I'm just a teeny bit busy, and maybe you could torture one of *six other assistants* instead of throwing more work at me?"

I checked my watch. "George and I are going to leave for

lunch in less than a minute. I require these tasks to be finished upon our return thirty minutes from now."

Pam narrowed her big dark eyes. "Oh," she said slowly. She took a step backward but I was certain she had not realized it. "It's you. I thought—yeah. Sure, it'll be ready when you get back."

"Excellent." Pam rushed away, the fluorescents bouncing off her bald, stubbled head. She had one of the most aesthetically pleasing complexions I had ever seen, all dark skin with mahogany undertones, and the cheekbones of an Egyptian princess.

I stood, walked past the printer, and caught George at the elevators. "Lunch," I ordered, and he sensibly complied.

Chapter Fifty-one

George stared at the innocuous-appearing, environmentally unfriendly plastic foam take-out box, and at the cheap chopsticks and black plastic utensils gripped in my fist.

"Is that it, Shiro?" His voice was hushed; he was looking at the take-out equivalent of the Ark of the Covenant. When I had explained my culinary mission, he abandoned all hope of Culver's frozen custard and accompanied me. "Is that actually it?"

"It is," I confirmed, restraining myself from stroking the box. I had been on a mission for decent duck for several years. Then, a few weeks ago, the hideously named Lotus Garden EZ Take 'N' Go had hired a new chef who was getting rapid local attention for his Roast Duck with Apples, a dish the *Pioneer Press* dubbed "ambrosia in a soggy carton."

I have a couple of weaknesses, gustatory curiosity being one. Thus, I determined to have ambrosia in a soggy carton before the first snowfall. And now it was mine.

We were almost back at headquarters, where I planned to savor my lunch at my desk while studying files. The smell coming out of the box was beyond heavenly—almost beyond imagining. Ahhhh, duck.

George shook his head. "I'm not believing you dropped twenty bucks for a retarded chicken."

I ignored him.

"We should've gone to Culver's. Ah, shit."

"Stop whining."

"I've got a lot to whine about—and so do you." As we walked through the lobby I saw what George had seen first: Frick and Frack had stepped from the elevator banks and were headed straight for us.

I suddenly felt very protective toward my duck. My grip tightened on the doggy bag holding the soggy carton.

"Awwww, if it in't the loving couple," Frack oozed.

"Didja enjoy your noon quickie?"

I answered them with a cordial "Shut up."

They traded glances. "Hey, we're not judgin'. So who are you now? You're the weapons expert now, arencha?"

"And you care why, precisely?"

"*We* got seniority," the other one said. "We're next up and we got this goddamned fraud case while you're chasin' psychos."

"Takes one to catch one," Frack jeered, an interesting comment from a confirmed kleptomaniac and arsonist. A thief with impulse control who likely wet the bed until he was twenty-four, in other words. "How come Michaela dumped ThreeFer on you?"

"Ask Michaela," George suggested. "She loves it when guys second-guess her."

Frack then did an incredibly stupid thing, even for him: he reached out and grabbed George's horrific tie and yanked.

Would have yanked. I dislocated his thumb before he could complete the move.

"Aw," George said happily over Frack's drilling shriek. "I didn't know you cared, Shiro."

"I do not." This was nothing but the truth. However, I needed to stop this chain of threats before it started. If these bullies felt comfortable reaching for George's tie, they would feel comfortable reaching for my duck. And my duck was inviolate. Preventative violence was the most efficient answer here.

As Frack thrust his wounded hand between his thighs and hunched over in pain, Frick suddenly pushed past his partner until we were almost chest to chest.

"You fuckin' make me sick, you crazy bitch. Walkin' around here like your shit don't stink. You're nothing in a real fight, Shiro. I wish I could see you take someone on without all that fancy Jew-jitsu shit, you won't last two—"

Without dropping my duck, I swung a right hook into his nose, switched the doggy bag to the other hand, followed up with a left cross, and then smashed him across the lower jaw with the back of the same fist. He crashed spectacularly into the receptionist's desk, and I heard several things break. Her mouse. Her computer screen. Her collection of tiny crystal dolphins. His lower left ribs.

"Wish granted."

"Say hi to the ER attending for us," George added.

I stepped past them to get back to work, George on my heels like an evil puppy.

Chapter Fifty-two

About thirty minutes later, I glanced up to see Pam with the work I had given her. She had changed out of her green-and-white sushi pajamas and into her pink-and-black poodle set. Not much of an improvement.

"Your witness is here."

I arched my eyebrows and picked my teeth with a tiny duck wing bone. "Oh?"

"Tracy Carr? She said she needed to see you?"

I frowned but did not comment. I loathed it when people made statements into questions? Like that? Was that not pathetic?

"She didn't say exactly which one of you . . . er, your sisters, she wanted to speak to. Probably she doesn't know."

"Very well. I will come out and collect her momentarily."

I finished my notes for Cadence, tossed the bone in George's top drawer (where I found two more ties with disturbing dead-animal patterns), then went out to talk to Tracy Carr.

"Good afternoon."

She stood at once, the only one in the reception area besides the receptionist, whose name frequently escaped me (Cadence would know: she knew everybody's name, no matter how inconsequential—that woman was a genius at wasting time) and Opus, the floor's janitor. He was emptying the recycling bins in that methodical way of his, slowly answering Tracy Carr's questions.

I confess: I was surprised. Opus rarely engaged anyone. Cadence was developing a bit of a soft spot for him, and I could not say he had offended me during his time with us thus far. A withdrawn, disheveled, gentle giant of a man, he had been with us for nearly two years. He had no concept of small talk, time, or dates, but could name pi to the thousandth digit after the decimal in less than twenty minutes. I have seen many things, but if I had not seen that myself, I would never have believed it.

He answered questions from Tracy Carr—what was his morning like, where did he buy groceries, and so on—slowly and deliberately. To her credit, she did not stare or laugh or refuse to make eye contact; or was she overly bluff and hearty.

Refreshing.

She caught sight of me, gave Opus a farewell pat on the shoulder, and walked right over. "Hi. You wanted me to come in?"

"Yes."

"I'm here."

"Clearly."

Opus was standing in what I thought of as "his" way: shoulders slumped, head down, and quiet as a stone.

"Thank you for entertaining my guest," I said to him.

"I'm here."

"Yes."

He paused so long I assumed he had finished, and started to turn away. I turned back at his "She's here, too."

"Yes." I think I would have found this irritating had it been someone else. But I was not insensitive to his issues. He went out and found employment (or was recruited), which could not have been easy. Others would have chosen a simpler path. Others would have hidden from the world. And the world would not have noticed, or thanked them. "Thank you."

"Okay." He walked out with a stack of emptied bins.

"Do you think he'll be all right?"

A rude question, but courteously phrased. "He is perfectly fine within his parameters."

"Oh. That's good. Listen, I wanted to talk to you about supper. If you and I went for a coffee, I wouldn't need the bodyguard. And I've been thinking about what you said and you're right; it would do me good to socialize."

Cadence and her socializing! I had the courtesy to intervene when she got herself into physical confrontations; why could she not return the favor when she tossed out meal invitations like confetti?

Oh, good. Here she came.

Chapter Fifty-three

"So thanks," Tracy said, lifting her coffee.

"You're welcome. We should do this again sometime." I meant it—I had enjoyed the conversation with Tracy, who regaled me with polite and increasingly articulate questions: about why I liked coffee more than tea, why I loved my career, what sports teams I liked, and my colleagues at BOFFO—even Opus, whom I gathered she had talked with while Shiro was around.

"I'd like that." She winked. "I promise to ask fewer questions next time, and let you ask your share."

"Hey, no problem. Heaven knows I've asked you my share of questions already."

My phone rang. It was Michaela; even if I hadn't recognized her strained voice, the chopping sound in the background was a dead giveaway.

"Shiro Jones!"

"It's Cadence, boss."

"Yes, yes. Pam tells me you're off having coffee. If you're

done socializing with civilians, I thought you might get yourself to a crime scene."

"Well, not that you asked, but I'm actually working. I—wait. Is it—?" I cut myself off, noting Tracy's presence.

"It is. Your partner's already on the way. Move; he'll pick you up at Nicollet and Tenth."

I barely said a proper good-bye to Tracy, which made me feel bad. There was no excuse for being rude, no matter how quickly a serial killer was escalating. We didn't all have to be savages. At least, I used to think so.

Chapter Fifty-four

I had barely climbed in before George was pulling away from the curb; the door swung shut and nearly closed on my ankle. I jerked my foot out of the way without a word; time was definitely not on our side.

But I had to complain when he threw a large wad of crinkly paper straight at my face.

"What the—?"

"It came about two seconds before we caught the squeal. Who's the asshole?"

It wasn't a wad of crinkly paper. Well, it was, but it was paper wrapped around what appeared to be three hundred purple irises. George took the next corner at roughly the speed of sound, so I was squashed against my door when I tried to find a card.

Never mind the card; my life was in danger. I clawed for my seat belt and, after way too long, heard the comforting click.

"I have no—" There it was, the little sneaky card. I grabbed for it, missed as George stomped the accelerator to catch the light, swiped again, missed as he whipped over to the far left lane (aaggh! this wasn't England!), then finally got my hands on it.

"To my three favorite girls—let's try it again."

"Barf," was my partner's comment.

"He certainly is brave," I admitted, secretly pleased. "Also persistent. It's a known quality when dealing with bakers."

"Oh. Your friend's wack-job brother."

"No, my friend's quite normal brother. Your trouble, George, is that you see wack jobs everywhere."

He didn't bother to respond, not that I could blame him. The truth was the truth, after all.

"So'd you jump him or what? No, wait—course you didn't. Guys don't spend a hundred bucks on flowers if they've already gotten laid."

"That's not—" Wait. He was right. Um.

"So you should keep 'em crossed until he coughs up something better than dying plant life. Hold out for jewelry," Dr. Love counseled, "or plane tickets. Then claw his back and beg for the big hairy banana. Or any hairy banana, I s'pose—is he a big guy? Tall? Big hands? Because you can usually tell if they're—"

"I may puke, and this is a new record, George—I've been exposed to you for only twenty seconds."

"If you puked as often as you said you might puke, you'd be fifteen pounds lighter."

"You're in a mood," I observed.

"I'm sick of this fucker. I'd like a night off from his pathetic shit. Just one night. Why'd he escalate in our fucking town?"

"He definitely should have checked with you first."

I don't know why I bothered. Sarcasm was almost always lost on him, and this time was no exception.

I sniffed my flowers and tried to remember the last time someone had sent me irises. Of course. Cathie—on my last birthday. She must have told Patrick irises were my favorite.

It was absurd, but I was actually cheering up a little despite being en route to a murder scene.

Minutes later, I sighed as George pulled into the nearest parking spot. Had I been so silly to say I loved crime scenes? Shiro was right; I *was* an idiot.

I stared out the window and decided I hated crime scenes. Particularly when the bad guys escalated and body after body kept showing up.

Yes. Definitely. Hate them.

Hate them.

Chapter Fifty-five

I carelessly tossed the vegetation in the backseat and looked over the scene. I knew Cadence did not care for crime scenes, despite what she told others—despite what she told herself. As for myself, I appreciated the efficiency most law enforcement officials showed at these locales. There was not a lot of bluster or turf battling, and virtually no socializing.

On the other hand, I disliked getting blood all over the bottoms of my shoes.

I assessed the scene and determined there was no danger to Cadence. Why had she

Chapter Fifty-six

"—showed up, don't you think?"

I blinked and glanced at my watch. In the short time I'd been gone, George had parked and gotten out of the car, crossed to my window, and rapped on it. And thrown my flowers into the backseat, the pitiless bum. His tie—drawn and quartered penguins—flapped in the wind.

"Huh?"

"Hey! Wake up!" Then he pressed his mouth against the glass and inflated, fogging it and distorting his face so that he looked like an angry bullfrog. "We got work!"

I sighed and got out. The place was already teeming with dozens of techs, cops, and agents. Dozens more reporters were held back behind the tape line. Poor guys, they were only trying to make a living. I sure hated seeing them back there waving mikes and lugging cameras.

Several of them saw George and me approaching, guessed correctly that we had a role here (or perhaps even recognized us from past ThreeFer scenes), and rushed us with a blitz of questions and

Chapter Fifty-seven

Flashes really bother me. Each photographic flare looks, sounds, and feels like something stealing your dignity. Which is really what is happening, if you think about it. People reduced to images. Professionals on scene, stripped of their thoughts and voices. Clothed pornography.

The ratings-obsessed panderers to society's idiot box crowded George and me like a pack of rabid bloodhounds, baying and howling and waving microphones.

It was sickening. There they were, skulking behind the First Amendment and excusing atrocious behavior by claiming the public had a right to know.

The public had a right to know, indeed. It had a right to know what we—the government—knew would actually inform it, be of use to it. Nothing more; nothing less.

An ambulance pulled up and they started squealing like piglets, waving and pushing and shouting. The temptation to reach out and break a few noses was getting more and more difficult to ignore. I stormed past them, hitting my shoulders against cameras, deciding my presence here did more harm than

Chapter Fifty-eight

"Good, you're here!"

I blinked; I was just past the line of photographers and reporters who had rushed me, just in front of the house. It was a nondescript starter home, white with red shutters, a roughly tended yard, and a modest "two-car" garage, if your cars were bicycles.

"I didn't think you were ever going to come."

It was Detective Clapp, and he looked ghastly. I'm sure I did, too. This triad-obsessed jerk was running everyone ragged.

"C'mon, you gotta come in, come in here!"

"Clapp, you're gonna stroke out if you don't take a pill." George studied Clapp's pupils and smelled the man's breath. "Holy shit! How many Frappuccinos have you had?"

"I lost count after eight."

Wow. Detective Clapp was actually vibrating. I'd never seen him like this before, and the man loved coffee like astronauts loved oxygen.

"Do we have another live victim?" I asked, preparing to be relieved.

"No. Come on. Come on!"

"All right, Detective. It's all right," I lied. At this time, nothing was all right. "Go ahead, we're here, lead the way."

"Right. Right! Okay! Come in!"

George and I traded glances and shared a rare moment of mutual understanding. Clapp had no idea he was screaming.

What was in that house? And oh God, why was I approaching?

"Wow," George muttered as we followed the detective through the house and toward what was apparently a back bedroom. "Maybe we should call him an ambulance."

"He'll be all right," I said doubtfully. I was a little cheered to see there were no signs of violence anywhere. A false alarm? A copycat? One ThreeFer crime scene that wasn't awful and gory and staged? Maybe this wouldn't be so bad.

But George was rattled, which made me terribly nervous. George hadn't even noticed Jerry Nance in the kitchen, meticulously picking through cupboards, sinks, and the fridge. God knew how many condiments he'd smuggled into his handmade pockets.

"Oh my fucking *God,*" George gasped, stopping so suddenly I ran into him.

I opened my mouth to scold him for being unprofessional, and then I saw what he did and slammed my teeth together so hard I almost amputated the tip of my tongue.

A bedroom. Pastel walls. Furniture by HOM. A door leading to what I assumed was a closet. Three victims. Three *women*—that was new. My nostrils involuntarily flared at the heavy, nauseating smell of fresh blood. And although the bedspread was soaked with blood, the three bodies were propped up against the far wall, held standing I don't know how and holding hands.

A tall, lean blonde.

A petite Asian American woman.

A muscular, leggy redhead.

And above them, written in blood, one word:

SOON.

I was going to puke. Or faint. Or faint then puke. Gritting my teeth wasn't going to stop it. Slitting my own throat wasn't going to stop it. He knew me, he knew my sisters, he knew about us, he knew our secret, and oh my God, what was going on here, oh please God, please please tell me what

what

Very faintly, I heard George's voice. Odd. He sounded . . . alarmed? No. Scared. How very, very

"Oh, shit! She's gonna blow!"

odd.

"—back! Everybody get back right now! *Don't touch her!*"

what

no oh no

what

(Daddy watch out! The goose, Daddy, the gooooooose!)

"WHAT IS GOING ON HERE?" I screamed, and then fell backward into a blood-covered tunnel that rapidly widened.

Believe me, I was happy to go.

Chapter Fifty-nine

I looked at the wall and could not bring myself to judge Cadence. She just was not up to this kind of stress and never had been.

Poor Cadence.

Poor me.

"Uh . . ." George was creeping forward. "Shiro?"

"Yes." Sighs of relief from all over the room; I almost smiled. Our reputations preceded us. "For now." Everybody tightened up again. "I see now why you were so anxious for us to get here," I told Detective Clapp, who looked like he was going to jump out of his Men's Wearhouse suit at the first opportunity.

I turned to George. "Perhaps it is time to work?"

So we did.

Chapter Sixty

"You got *any* idea what this means?" a tech asked me. We were bonneted and booteed, collecting evidence and taking pictures and doing the thousand other jobs a crime scene entailed.

"Not yet," I replied. I was always privately amused at how relieved most techs were to see me, as opposed to Cadence. Her admitted charm could be exhausting. All the techs I had ever met had a very orderly and linear way of looking at the world; they did not want pep talks and charm. They wanted facts.

I was usually able to provide them. But at this time, I had only the vaguest suspicions.

I read the newest sonnet, which had been left on top of the dresser.

"O truant Muse, what shall be thy amends/For thy neglect of truth in beauty dyed?/Both truth and beauty on my love depends;/So dost thou too, and therein dignified."

The sonnets, puzzling and odd before, had a decidedly sinister tone to me now.

They were love notes, I finally realized.

Notes to my sisters and me.

ThreeFer had been speaking to me since the very first crime scene, from two states away.

Now he was here. In my city. In our home.

"He will regret this," I muttered. "He will see how stupid it was to leave a trail. How very childish and stupid."

"Attagirl," George said. "You can make him squeal like a piglet when you catch up to him; that'll make you feel better."

"It will," I agreed, actually smiling at him.

After rereading through the file earlier, I had begun to wonder if our killer might not be a multiple personality. This bold stroke, this crime scene which all but called us by name, suggested he (or she) knew far more about us than we did about him.

But please. Please do not be a cop, or a fed. I hate dirty cops. And dirty feds gave us all a bad name.

As they began to zip up the bodies, I walked over, raised my eyebrows in a question, and then unzipped each of the three bags. I peeled back eyelids with my thumb and observed that the eye colors, in addition to the builds, nationalities, and colorings of my sisters and me, were also dead on.

Huh. I squatted beside the bodies, absently letting go of the last victim's eyelid and watching it slowly roll back down.

Interesting.

Chapter Sixty-one

Patrick called while I was still on the scene. I kept the call short, perhaps too much so. It was not my intention to be rude or to ruin Cadence's love life; there was simply nothing to be done about it. The work had to come first.

Nevertheless, I was surprised at how disappointed I was. The man had infuriated me with his antics that night outside Ottavio's. Of course, he had infuriated all three of us, albeit for different reasons.

About four hours later, I was finally home and in the grip of a throbbing headache. Words were blurring together and I was heartily sick of crime-scene photos—not to mention the crime scene itself. My duck had been hours ago and I was cobbling together an evening snack of iced coffee and steamed rice.

I closed the refrigerator door, then stiffened as I heard someone walking down the hallway outside. The person paused just outside my apartment door.

Oh, lovely. I hoped it was the killer. This would all be over soon if I could just get my hands around his neck. Soon, but not quickly. No, I would not make it quick, because he had frightened my sister so badly. It would last and last and

Chapter Sixty-two

Last one on the bus is a rotten egg and a dead killer!
Yes yes!
It's the killer round and round
Round and round
Round and round

> *(How stupid is the killer*
> *round and round*
> *to come*
> *to my*
> *house!)*
>
> *(Oh you can come in*
> *Please do come in*
> *Come on in!)*

Yes, the killer can walk right in

Walk right in
Walk right in

(I'm coming, killer!   Don't go away!   Wait for me! Waitwait!)

And I'll hit him
And I'll bite

And scratch
And blow his house down

I am at the door!   I am unlocking it
Why is the door locked?

(stupid Shiro so cautious and dull she is squashed
Squashed inside us
flat and dull but she's sleeping now sleeping
Shhhhhh)
And now the door is open
And I can see
I can see
I can see
The door is open and one-two-three

It's the Pillsbury Doughboy!

(Oh well perhaps the killer will come by later
I'm glad the Dough Boy is here!

glad
glad
glad)

(and I jumped on him because he smells like food
And now ka-boom!)
Pillsbury Doughboy is on his back
On his back
On his back
(Oh, the look! The look on your face! Such pretty eyes,
yesyes! Pretty like my sister's
The scared one
The

(Cadence)

Now we're in the hallway
Round and round
And boy does he look stunned

The wheels on the bus go round and round,
he
smells
like
food!

And I am kissing him
Kissing him
Kissing him

I'm kissing him
But
Now
I'm
Bored.

He's not the killer.
Meh.

Chapter Sixty-three

Of all the places my sisters had left me, this one was new: right on top of a guy. And in my own apartment, no less! Patrick's face and mine were not even six inches apart.

"Ah. Hmm. How long have we been like this?"

"Three hours. You were insanely good."

"What?"

He burst out laughing and twisted his hips, heaving me off him. I realized then we both still had our clothes on. "Okay, three seconds. But they sure were memorable."

"What are you doing here?"

"You blew me off on the phone."

Must've been Shiro, busy at work. "Yes, well, that means we *don't* have time to talk. And yet here you are, deciding it's okay to ignore my wishes—"

"Your sister's wishes. I knew you'd feel differently, Cadence."

This irritated me even more. "So your new game is to play us against each other? How is that romantic, exactly?"

He clambered to his feet, moving quickly for such a large man, and extended a hand. I ignored it and stood on my own.

"I don't mean I came here for action," he said. "I came here to make sure you take care of yourself. Cathie told me that when you're using your powers to fight evil, you forget to eat. So . . . now where the hell is it?" He looked around, clearly distracted, and I couldn't help notice the beautiful cut of his suit (Italian, I was sure), the shadow of stubble on his face, the mesmerizing eyes. Yes indeed, it was a shame that work had to come before pleasure.

"Adrienne knocked me right over on my back when she shot out the door. I must've—aha!" He scooped up a sloppy cardboard container, and just when I had decided my liking for him had a ceiling, he handed it to me. It was filled with roast duck. "Cathie said you—Shiro you, not all of you—she said you were trying to find time to order this."

"Thanks for this. I'm afraid I can't let you stay," I said, unable to keep the genuine regret out of my tone. "There are classified documents all over my apartment." Not to mention several repulsive photographs.

"That's all right. I'm just glad to see you. Any of you—even if it's just for a few seconds."

"Adrienne didn't—didn't hurt you?"

"No. She knocked me over and told me I smelled like food. Then she sang that nursery rhyme 'The Wheels on the Bus.' Just as I was about to start singing along, she left."

He had gotten off lightly. Again. Was it possible that all *three* of us were getting fond of him?

"Thank you for stopping in. It was very kind of you to bring me another duck."

"Another—?"

"Never mind. Thank you again. And, um . . . I'm sorry I punched your lights out."

He rubbed his jaw. "Aw, that? That was nothing. A love tap."

"My first, on a first date anyway. What time'd you wake up?"

"About an hour later."

"You're just saying that."

"You're right. It was about five minutes. Still impressive."

"Thanks. Um, you'll please see yourself out?"

"I never made it in," he said, sarcastically. But he softened the gripe with another heart-stopping grin. "Fine, go on. Catch bad guys."

"Oh yes," I said, opening my door. "Count on it."

"Cool."

I was still smirking like a fool. And long after he'd gone, I still couldn't stop smiling.

Chapter Sixty-four

I found myself sitting at my kitchen table, my head pillowed on my arms. I blinked—morning sunshine was streaming into the room. I was sore all over my back and neck. And *ravenous*.

Boy. Boy oh boy, I didn't think I'd ever been so happy to be a multiple than I was when I was able to escape that nightmare of a bloody bedroom. I decided to leave Shiro (at least I hope it was Shiro) a thank-you note. She inevitably tossed them into our fireplace, but still. It was the thought that counted.

I went to the fridge and grabbed the first thing I saw—a Coke. I chugged it in about four belch-inducing swallows, then heard the phone ring. I plunked the can on the counter and looked at the caller ID: Cathie.

"Hey there," I answered. "What's up?"

"Cadence? Is that you?"

"Hi, Patrick. I thought you were Cathie."

"Yeah, I'm at her apartment right now. Listen, are you all right?"

"Sure." Odd. He sounded worried. But about what? "Are *you* all right? You sound stressed."

"I am stressed! You promise you're okay."

"What's going on?"

"What's going on is that I haven't seen you in forever."

"That's sweet," I said, remembering the way he smiled at me just outside the apartment.

"No, seriously. I'm worried. I've knocked on your door, called, texted you . . . nothing. The only thing that stopped me from dialing 911 was calling your work number that Cathie gave me. Your boss told me to stop being such an overbearing male influence or she'd flay my privates. Charming woman. But at least I was reasonably sure you were alive. Where've you been?"

I shook my head. "Patrick, are you messing with me? I just saw you last night. Woke up on top of you after Adrienne tackled you, accepted your peace offering of duck . . ."

"Um, Cadence." The pause was disturbing. "That was three nights ago."

I nearly dropped the phone. "Three nights?" Rats! That would explain my exhaustion. And soreness. And appetite. "Golly, what happened?"

He sighed. "I was hoping you'd know."

I spotted what I'd been too thirsty and hungry to see when I woke up: files neatly stacked on my table, and several pages of notes in Shiro's precise handwriting. Also, daily newspapers from the last three days.

"Ah. Okay. I see. Um, Patrick, I'm fine. Thanks for calling. I've gotta go."

"But—"

"Patrick, if it's been three days, I'm way behind on work. And I've got a killer to catch. And I think I missed Tina's party, holy old rat guts!"

"You're so weird."

"Glad you've been paying attention. I promise to make it up to you. Give Cathie a hug for me."

I hung up on him before he could protest, sat back down, reached for the top page of Shiro's notes, and began to read.

Chapter Sixty-five

Cadence,

First, my regrets for your extended absence. I had a great deal of work to do. I have been able to pull some information together which I hope might assist you in our investigation. As you will see by the end, I cannot go any further myself. The time has come for you to finish putting the pieces together.

As you already deduced, I have found numerous examples of the number three throughout the ThreeFer file. Where we erred was assuming the instances of three were him/her telling us about him/her. I now think he/she has been telling us about . . . us.

I now strongly suspect he (I do not feel the nonzero chance of a female suspect warrants further consideration, so will in the future refer to ThreeFer as he) suffers from our common affliction, MPD.

I grimaced and resisted the urge to crumple Shiro's note into a teeny tiny ball. This just got more and more awful.

I have prepared condensed files for you from the last crime scene. Knowing too much detail would upset you for personal reasons, I had George edit certain aspects of the material and focus only on those elements that truly matter. Three points I must make:

1. *George still whines like a crippled camel when the case lead assigns him work. This is inefficient. Please put your persuasive "people skills" to good use, and ask Michaela to assign him elsewhere.*

2. *Beyond the obvious nature of the deaths, there is very little at the crime scene that indicates reckless violence. The blood is contained to the bedroom area, and mostly the bed itself, and as you know we have puzzled over the lack of defensive wounds on the victims, suggesting some emotional bond between the murderer and the victims—or possibly between the murderer and us.*

3. *The murderer used large spikes to keep the bodies standing against the wall . . . but as you will see from these edited photographs, he did not nail the bodies there, but rather propped them up. Strange, given that they were already dead, that he would not simply mutilate them further to get the proper pose. He risked having them fall off the spikes, rather than hurt the bodies further.*

I took some time with this information before reading further. Shiro was surprised by not just the artistry and care, but something approaching tenderness. Tenderness implied familiarity. Familiarity implied . . . acquaintance, or worse.

Barf.

You will also notice I have left morning editions of the local papers for you. They include some real-estate offers, and I have followed up with some deals on the Internet. See the attached printouts—in particular, the one highlighted in blue.

It took time to find this one, and I am afraid I needed George's assistance to contact the local police from some out-of-state locales. Apparently, Michaela feels his phone manner is better than mine. I did monitor his calls to ensure he would ask the correct questions.

These calls confirmed that one of our very few witnesses, the gentleman from the Pierre scene, has since moved to Minneapolis. You will recall Mr. Scherzo was the man who found the Pierre bodies and called the local police. He is here now, a strong coincidence. I suggest you alert Michaela and then interview this witness once more. Only you have the skills necessary to conduct the interview properly, so that his suspicions are not too quickly aroused. His current address, as you will find in the 297B file, is 369 Tarragon Way.

By now you may have come to the same conclusions I have

Thanks, Shiro; usually you assume I'm still foundering in ignorance.

but in case you have not,

Oh, great. Guess I got ahead of myself.

I shall say it simply: If this man is not the killer, he knows the killer. And the killer, whoever he is, knows us.

Good gosh, she really thought I was an imbecile!

I looked at the clock and gasped. *No time to waste!* I ran out of the apartment so quickly, I was all the way to my car before I realized I was barefoot, and in a T-shirt and panties.

It must be Tuesday.

Chapter Sixty-six

The house was in a somewhat rough neighborhood in North Minneapolis—the type that looked better by day than by night, despite the peeling paint on every aging house and broken machinery on every unkempt lawn. Scherzo's was a bit neater than average: pale green with a high chain-link fence surrounding the carefully mowed crabgrass.

There was a BEWARE OF DOGS sign at the front gate, but a quick visual check down either side of the house revealed nothing. Same with a rattling of the gate and a loud "Hello." Dogs were probably inside.

I unlatched the gate and stepped up the cobblestone path to the door, taking in the low-maintenance pebble-and-bush garden and three-season porch that fronted the house.

Just as my hand touched the latch to the porch door, three Dobermans came whipping around the corner.

They weren't inside, I told myself, freezing in terror at their size and speed. *They were hiding in back. They were quiet. And they were well trained. Now they're going to have me for a*

Chapter Sixty-seven

SNACK ON THIS, BITCHES!

BAM!

KA-POW!

BAM-BLOOIE!

Just like in the old Batman *television show! Holy hot dogs, Batman! Batgirl saves the day!*

Damn.

Puppies can take a hit.

Okay fine

Get up

You too

You three

Growl growl growl

(honk honk honk)

Let's go again

This time

Animal

To

Animal

Chapter Sixty-eight

That was fun.
Not even close
To bored yet.
What was I doing here?
Besides killing dogs.
Who cares.
Let's go
Have some
FUN
Lessee
Lots of houses
But no bars
Where can a girl get a guy to buy her a drink?
Need wheels.
Need to go round and round.
Need to fly.
Need to flap my wings.

Need to . . . dance!
Dancing in the street till it ain't no thing,
Can I get a "what-what" from the dead doggie section!
WHAT-bark!
WHAT-yip!
WHAT-crack!
Thank you, hound-homies!
Give a ghost-puppy snack to the spines that went
CRRRRRRRAAAAAAAAACK
Walking too far
(This is almost boring)
Whom does a girl have to FUCK
To get a drink around here?
WOOOT THERE IT IS
ON THE CORNER
Of the street
Where a bus
Goes round
Liquor store!
Liquor store!
Liquor store!
Tell me more!
Tell me do you have
A beer
A lonely, lovely beer
Something I can wrap my lips around and kill
FUCK!

Who closes their goddamn liquor store first thing in the morning? Not me. Not my liquor store. No, when I have a liquor store I'm gonna run it MY way. I'm gonna SMASH the window when I want to get in, CLIMB through and apparently KNOCK OVER a display or two on my way in, RUN down the aisle

WHEEEEEE FREE AS A GOOSE

And then SMASH the door to the refrigerator unit in the back, REACH in, and GRAB. THAT. BEER.

Yep. It's gonna be just like this. Except I'm not going to have that fucking alarm going off.

Damn it. Alarm. I didn't pay for my drink.

And why

Should I?

Should a girl like me pay for her own drinks?

NO.

Not a damn decent man around here who'll do it.

I need to call a man.

I need

To call

PILLSBURY!

Chapter Sixty-nine

I woke up in Patrick's SUV, which smelled rudely of alcohol and vomit.

Judging from the bites and scratches on my arms, not to mention the split skin and shards of glass all over my fists and wrists, I assumed I had a much more serious wound somewhere I could not feel. *I'm in shock,* I told myself. *Great. Dead by Doberman at twenty-seven. Life is too rich.*

But wait. Why was I in Patrick's SUV instead of an ambulance? What was he even—

"You okay back there?" He turned briefly to verify I was awake. "Cripes, Adrienne. You could have told me you needed to yark. I would've stopped."

My blood froze. "Adrienne was here?"

"Adrienne was everywhere."

"How did you find her . . . I mean, me?"

"She called me. Gave me the address: 369 Tarragon Way. I went there, found some dead dogs, heard the alarm blasting down the street, followed the sound, and saw a bit of a crowd gathering around the liquor store."

I closed my eyes and prayed for death.

"No one wanted to go in, and they figured the police would take another good forty or fifty minutes to show, since you weren't moving and no one was in imminent danger. I slipped in through the window you busted, found you unconscious at the back with a dead case of Sam Adams and a half-empty bottle of Grey Goose vodka, and dragged you out the fire door . . . which, no doubt, would have triggered the alarm, had one not already been blaring. Brought you back to the car and drove away. Um, Cadence . . . someone may have taken down my license plate."

God, as usual, was ignoring my prayers. "Don't worry about it. Michaela will make sure this disappears." *After she pulls my left boob into a phallic shape and cuts it off. Good golly, Adrienne! Could you have left me in a bigger mess? And I'll bet you didn't even check inside the house after you killed those dogs. Not that it would have been any better if you had.*

"We need to go back," I told Patrick.

"You need to go to a hospital first."

I looked over my wrists and started picking out the glass. It hurt. Also, there was probably some rabies protocol I would be wise to follow. "Fine. Hospital first. But then we need to go back."

"Mmm."

"Thanks for the flowers," I remembered.

Patrick smiled at me. "Adrienne thanked me first. I had no idea she liked irises. I mean, literally liked them. She likes to eat them."

"No, she likes to turn virtually anything she can into a straw, through which she sips vodka. That's what she likes." And here came the hangover I didn't deserve, right on cue.

"Uh, no offense, hon—"

I braced myself.

"Is your boss really going to cover this up? A federal agent breaking and entering? Destruction of property, public drunkenness?"

"Mm-hmm." Was that—it was! I spat out a purple iris petal. "The government needs us."

"Because you're really good at your job?"

"Because we do what most people can't. And we keep doing it. We keep showing up, and wading through blood and guts, we keep chasing the *really* crazy people, the ones who really would just as soon kill you—or a nurse, or a child, or a father, or a waitress—as look at you."

"Your incredibly stressful and dangerous government work can't drive you crazy," Patrick guessed, "because you already are."

"Well. Yes."

Patrick chuckled and accelerated. "It makes as much sense as anything the government does, I suppose." He peeked at me, a glance full of warmth and teasing affection. "Certainly hiring you makes more sense than trying to rewrite the tax code for the zillionth time."

I spit out another blossom and laughed; I couldn't help it.

Chapter Seventy

The hospital visit was routine, in that I went from curtained area to curtained area without any information or courtesy until they were done poking and prodding and bandaging me. They kept Patrick confined to the waiting area, so we didn't even get to talk. Instead, I used the time to check in with Michaela, advise her of what had happened, listen to her urge Opus out of her office, since "this was no time to be emptying wastebaskets when my best agent's hurt," make her call Opus back in so the poor man could do his job, assure her I was okay, assure her a man hadn't done this to me, plead with her not to go castrate someone anyway, hush the nurses who tried to tell me not to use cell phones in this area, apologize profusely to the nearby patients whose heart monitors chose that moment to go berserk from cell interference, turn the cell phone off, apologize to the nurses for not listening, ask them for a landline, suffer their silent treatment for a while, plead with them for a landline, call Michaela again, apologize for cutting her off earlier, get her to agree to clear Patrick's license plate with the authorities, refuse Michaela's offer of assistance for my return visit to Scherzo's house, and apologize one last time to the nursing staff.

With all that activity, after which Patrick insisted we get lunch (drive-through Arby's), it wasn't until that afternoon that we got back to the house. I insisted Patrick stay in the SUV—frankly, I would have liked to see him go home, since my own car was still parked on the street. But it being a free country and all, the most I could do was get him to promise to stay in his vehicle and keep a cell phone handy. (No heart monitors in the neighborhood, I supposed.)

The dogs were still dead on the front lawn. All had spines broken backward to the point where they made nearly comical U shapes in the crabgrass. Flies dotted their broken teeth.

"Bless it," I breathed.

I had my hand on the porch door—darn it, I really had to stop doing that—when I heard the sound of smashing furniture. It was coming from inside.

Chapter Seventy-one

A bit surprised I was still there—usually Shiro would have jumped in at this point—I barged through the door and porch and, entering the living area, saw the shape of a large man bursting out the back door. I had no time to take in any features before I saw something worse: Jeremy Scherzo, our witness from South Dakota who had recently moved here, lying on the floor and bleeding profusely from the head.

I scrambled back to the porch and called out to Patrick to call 911 and tell them a federal agent was on the scene. Then I rushed back to Jeremy's side. When I did, I was relieved.

"Dj-dj-is he still here?"

I gave a small smile at the sight of his eyes opening. A quick mental recall of local police and BOFFO notes reminded me that the man was easily excitable and had a slight stutter. "No. He left. I don't think he'll be back."

"Yi-yi-he's been calling me. Threatening me. I think it's the same guy."

"What do you remember about him?" I looked over his

scalp. The wound appeared superficial but was still bleeding. I pulled off my windbreaker and used it to apply pressure.

"Big. Sh-sh-strong. He surprised me. Tried to t-t-choke me from behind."

"What did he use?"

Jeremy shrugged. "Soft. My-my-maybe rope. I got my finger underneath and we-we-when I didn't die, he tossed it and just sh-sh-started pummeling me."

Seeing him point vaguely to a corner, I turned to look. He'd left evidence. Unintentional evidence! Then my heart froze.

Coiled randomly in the corner, like a snake with no fashion sense, was a piece of cloth featuring a pattern of pink and purple hippos laced with the bloody crimson marks of vivisection.

It was a necktie.

Chapter Seventy-two

"Michaela, you've got to lock down George!" I was outside Scherzo's house; the paramedics were there; local officers (including Lynn and Jim) were taking my direction; and Patrick was suitably impressed at the moving parts I was controlling on the scene. All in all, pretty sexy.

You know, besides the guy bleeding from his head, and the dead U-dogs on the lawn.

And, um, the escaped serial killer.

But not for long. George's days were numbered.

"This is impossible," Michaela was trying to tell me, but I heard the doubt in her voice. "George has been through background checks and therapy—"

"You mean, the same background checks and therapy that tell us he's a sociopath capable of extreme violence to satisfy his God complex?"

"He attacks only skinheads and bigots."

"Well shucks, boss, maybe all the victims are bigots!" How

could she be so obtuse? Wasn't George a man? Didn't he have a penis? *She should be on board with this.*

"Next to you, he's our most consistently performing agent. . . . Cadence, this could shut BOFFO down. We need to be careful. And preferably quiet."

I almost drop-kicked the cell phone. "Fine—be careful. Be quiet. But LOCK HIM DOWN, BITTY-BIPSTER!"

Then I hung up.

Chapter Seventy-three

After asking Lynn to drive my car home, putting Jim and the other agents onto George (well, phooey on Michaela and her careful and her quiet!), and sending Patrick on his way, I rode in the ambulance with Jeremy.

I could tell after a quick check with the EMTs that his wounds were minor and he'd likely be released later that day. More than anything, he was upset about the dogs.

"She's k-k-gonna be pissed," was the sobbing reply when I asked about them.

"She?"

"They're ln-ln-not mine. My sister's. She's in the area, but she's been moving. I offered t-t-to watch them. They like me. Liked me, I mean."

I almost cried. "I'll bet they did. I'm so sorry about that. Did you see who killed them—was it the same man?"

He stared at me, and for a chilling moment I was sure he had seen the whole thing and was going to accuse my sister

Adrienne. But then, he let loose with a ferocious sneeze, and then a coughing fit, and the EMT applied an oxygen mask.

"We should probably let him calm down," she told me.

I agreed. Jeremy Scherzo had been through enough.

Chapter Seventy-four

Part of what got Patrick to leave the scene in North Minneapolis so quickly was a whispered promise to go out with him later. Being the stand-up kind of girl I am, I decided to follow through—this time, without the canceling and the honking and the slapping and the lecturing but maybe the kissing but definitely NOT the slugging.

That said, I almost did cancel when I got the call at home from Michaela.

"We can't find George."

"Sugar on a shingle!"

"You should be careful. I'd like to send a couple of agents out to—"

"No!" Not Frick and Frack! "I'll be fine. George probably knows I know, now. He's not going to come after me. He's running. If you have agent resources, put them there." I bit my lip. *Don't assign me tonight don't assign me tonight don't assign*

"All right. You've had quite a day, Cadence. Why don't you

rest. Call in every couple of hours and let us know you're okay."

I paused. "You're going to put a tail on me, aren't you?"

"Of course."

"Can I make a suggestion?"

Chapter Seventy-five

By the time Patrick showed up, our chaperones were ready.

"Patrick, I don't believe I had time earlier today to introduce two of my colleagues from the Minneapolis Police Department. This is Jimmy Clapp, and Lynn Rivers."

They were both off duty now and in dress casual clothes—the first time I'd ever seen either of them in dark jeans—and they both looked great. Lynn's black pumps really made a statement: her gun was *not* the most dangerous thing about her.

"Condition of the date," I hurriedly explained before Patrick could protest. "George Pinkman is still at large. My agency is worried about me, since I appear to be an . . . how do you say it, Jim?"

"Object of interest," he reminded me. I could tell he wasn't sure whether to sulk at the fact that I was going to have a date right in front of him, or take seriously the option of his fellow officer standing next to him, or shoot the only other male in the room and try to claim both women for himself. Ah, to be a testosterone-driven, hairy man. Decisions, decisions.

"Right. An object of interest to our suspect. Which I don't get. I mean, Patrick, do *you* see anything here that could represent any object of interest to a guy?" It was an outrageous flirt, but I was wearing my favorite red blouse and black jeans with red pumps, and I knew I was working it. These clothes were perfect for me—the jeans would have been too tall for Shiro's compact stature and the blouse too diaphanous for Adrienne's muscular frame—but despite what I knew would be their protests, I decided that since *I* was the one doing all the work of showering and dressing and makeup for this date, *I* was the one that was going to choose the outfit.

See, I realized, the black dress from the first date was too universal! My sisters could look fat or ridiculous this time, if they wanted to pop up. And good luck to them.

"Anyway, Cadence called Jimmy and me, and we're happy to help," Lynn finished explaining. "So where to?"

"I've reserved a table at the Mahogany Stallion," Patrick answered. "Er, the table was for two."

"Don't sweat it. If we have to, we'll flash our badges. That's good for a couple of extra chairs at most joints."

My date's nose wrinkled. "I don't know if they'd consider themselves a *joint*."

"Oh, stop being snooty. Jim and Lynn will be great company!" I truly believed this. I had been dying to spend time out of work with Lynn, and heck, I'd almost dated Jim! So how could this be bad?

Chapter Seventy-six

It was bad. Okay, it didn't involve physical violence like the last time, but it was still bad.

First, the maître d' at the Cherry Horse or Oak Duck or whatever the fig this restaurant called itself—well he did not take kindly to the doubling in size of our party. Apparently, the wineglasses and napkins and other bits of settings had already been "placed" for two, don't you know. He wasn't even impressed by the officers' badges (or my hints at federal authority). Those settings—they'd been PLACED. So that cost Patrick fifty bucks to fix.

Second, the chief of the Minneapolis police was there, and he recognized Lynn and Jim. Fraternizing among police officers, even in those police departments that allowed it, was not encouraged at all. So they had a great morning to look forward to the next day.

Third, Patrick was a bit of an ass.

"This bread is hard," he announced to the table shortly after we received our basket.

At first, I saw this as an opportunity to brag about him. "I don't know if you two knew, but Patrick is a baker. More than a baker—he runs the—"

"That's not my point. My point is, they're serving us stale bread! The maître d' must have talked to the kitchen."

Lynn frowned. "Why would he bother talking to the kitchen about us?"

"Because he's ticked that I showed up with twice as many people as I made the reservation for."

I reached for his hand. "I'm sure that's not it at—"

"Places like this get off on screwing with high-maintenance customers!" He moved his hand away. "Cadence, I know these things. I run in these circles. I don't expect you or your friends to understand."

That lowered the Curtain of Uncomfortable Silence upon us all for a good ten seconds.

Then, chewing my tongue, I offered: "Well, golly, Patrick. I'm sorry I don't understand your circle. Would you like me to try to find you a date who does?"

Jim cast a nervous glance over his shoulder at the chief's table. "I think he's with a woman who's not his wife."

Lynn shrugged. "Does that help us or hurt us?"

"I think it fucks us royally. Do you think they have any openings over in SPPD?"

"I don't know if I could do St. Paul. I hear the mayor there—"

"Guys, please don't worry." I gave them my best puppy eyes. "I'll talk to Michaela. She'll call your chief. She'll make sure he understands. I—"

"Where is our waiter?"

"I don't know, Patrick, but I'm sure he wasn't going to show up *before the end of my sentence.*"

"I gave that maître d' fifty bucks, and he fucked me."

"Yeah, well, he's the only one who's going to."

Finally, I'd got his attention. Unfortunately, I was met with a sneer. "Be serious. You were never going to, anyway. I'd have to get one of your sisters—"

"Waiter!" I called out desperately. Chiclets and Toblerone, I realized Patrick didn't know that Lynn and Jim didn't know my secret! How was I going to get him to shut up?

"I mean honestly, if you can just put yourself in one of those trances, you—"

"Jim and Lynn could you please go see if you can hunt down that super waiter I think I saw him at that table in the far corner thank you very much that's an awesome thing you're doin' there thanks."

Once they had gone, I grabbed his chin and looked deep into his eyes for mercy. "Okay. They don't know. You can't tell them."

He was momentarily confused, but caught on after a few seconds. "All right. What's it in for me?"

"I won't think you're a dirty skunk."

"Too late! You already think that. I want action."

"I'm not going to give myself up—"

"Nothing that serious." He considered. "Go down on me tonight."

I almost slapped him, but then remembered my promise to myself. "What, here?"

"No! Back at your apartment."

I shook my head. "I'll give you a really good kiss."

"You've already given me—"

"Without knocking you unconscious afterward."

"Hand job."

This wasn't happening to me. "I'll let you put your hand up my blouse."

He squinted.

I sighed. "And then I'll let you see me naked." Apparently I had been wrong; it was definitely happening to me.

"For a full minute."

"Ten seconds."

"Thirty."

"Twenty, and I'll lick a mirror." Where had I come up with that? Not to worry; it was too silly to be sexy. Patrick would never—

"Done."

"You are one twisted onion," I hissed at him as Jim and Lynn warily approached us with a waiter in tow.

Patrick kissed my wrist and winked. "*You're* the one that's going to strip and French yourself after I pinch your nipple."

"Good gravy, I can't believe I'm letting you touch me."

"Find a happy place. Pretend you're someone else."

"Hilarious."

Chapter Seventy-seven

It honestly wasn't that awful or embarrassing. Well okay, it was frightfully embarrassing. But he's the only one who saw it, and I think he'll keep his mouth shut.

I put honey on the mirror so it tasted nice, and Patrick was obviously turned on, and yet he was still gentleman enough to pick up his things to go when I ordered him out. So I gave him one more kiss on his way out the door. He grabbed my naked butt and threatened to pull me out into the apartment hallway, but I squealed and pulled away.

Giggling at his look of lust, I slammed the door in his face.

Still a virgin! Woo-hoo!

Chapter Seventy-eight

George was still at large the following morning when I got to work. I quickly briefed Michaela on the need to call the Minneapolis police chief (and perhaps congratulate him on his fine taste in streetwalkers), and then got down to business.

"Hey!" I shouted out to my electronic appointment book, where Pam had made some thoughtful additions. "I've got interviews with Jeremy and Tracy today!"

This felt good, starting a day without a whirlwind of sugar cubes. No new ThreeFer murders since George had almost been caught at Jeremy's, no new batches of paperwork to fill out because Adrienne had done something ridiculous the night before, no scheduled talks with Dr. Nessman . . . and no George at the office! Sure, seeing no George meant that he could still kill again; but on the other hand . . . no George at the office!

By the time the appointments with our two witnesses came up, I was humming a tune. Something classical—perhaps I had heard it in the elevator. I wasn't even sure at first . . .

"Hey, I know that one!" Tina was walking by with a copy of *EW*. " 'Nessun Dorma.' "

"Come again?"

" 'Nessun Dorma'? From Puccini's *Turandot*? Famous stuff. I didn't know you were an opera buff."

"I've never been to the opera." *Maybe Shiro has?*

She shrugged. "I guess you wouldn't have to. You'd just need one of the best-selling classical recordings of all time: *The Three Tenors in Concert*. Remember them? Pavarotti, and Domingo, and . . ."

"Yeah, yeah, the other one." *Huh. That is one of my favorite albums. . . . Did George know that? Is that why he stapled the poster to that victim's face?*

I was still ruminating on the possibilities when I entered the interview room. Conveniently enough, Jeremy and Tracy were in adjacent rooms. Each had a book of lay-downs, within which we had placed various photos of George with different configurations of facial hair and other disguising factors.

The tie and his flight from the law were probably enough to get and hold him; but we would need either a witness or DNA evidence to be sure we'd nail him. So far, Jeremy and Tracy looked like a far better bet than us finding a slipup by George. Good goat cheese, the guy's lawyer could argue that anything we found at a crime scene was there because . . . George was investigating every crime scene! Ugh, he'd had this all figured out long ago. We needed these witnesses to come through!

I tried not to let impatience and exasperation get the best of me. What would Shiro say?

Stop talking to yourself and get to work.

Hmmm. Not exactly the inspiration I was looking for.

Only you like these people enough to do this.

Better, but . . .

Your sister and I believe in you. Please help us.

Awright, sis! You bet I will! And I believe in you, too!

Two hours later, I left the interviewing area with absolutely nothing useful. Jeremy couldn't stop stuttering through nothing new, and Tracy was polite, distracted, and tapped out.

We were done. It was DNA or nothing.

Chapter Seventy-nine

I'd no sooner gotten back to my desk and picked my cell phone off my belt to call Lynn (did she still have a job?) when it buzzed in my hand like a big metal bee. I saw it was Cathie. "Hey. What's up?"

"What did you do to him?"

"Who?"

"Who do you think? My brother, jerk!"

I clutched the phone. "What? Is he hurt? What's wrong?"

"No, he's not hurt; he's moving here!"

"He's what?"

"Cadence, will you *please* clean the shit out of your ears so I don't have to keep repeating myself? My brother, the Emperor of Meringue, is house hunting in the Twin Cities. Never mind the location; the man's never lived in a *house*; he's a rental/hotel suite kind of guy."

"Maybe he's tired of all the traveling." I flipped through my e-mail as nonchalantly as I could. Maybe he had written me an e-mail looking for real-estate advice. Hmm. No. I was excited and pleased to hear Cathie's news, but cautioned myself that it likely had nothing to do with me.

"Patrick's just tired of being a nomad," I guessed.

"Did you give it up to him?"

I nearly dropped the cell. "Jeepers creepers' peepers, Cathie!"

"Don't fake swear at *me*. It was all I could think of. Either that, or you showed off the goods but wouldn't give it up. So he's buying a house to keep working you." There was a malignant pause. "Did you—one of you—strip for him?"

This was hitting way too close to home. "Cathie, why are you so interested in your brother's love life? Don't tell me the Irish Catholics don't frown on—"

"Yeah, okay, stop right there. My interest is one of sisterly love, for each of you. I'm not sure if you two dating is brilliant or ridiculous."

"Can it be both?"

"No. Only in a novel could it be both. This is real life. You have to choose one."

"Then it's brilliant."

"Damn it, Cadence, I was right. You let him see you naked. Did you strip? Did you put on 'You Can Leave Your Hat On'? Did you leave your hat on when you played it? And maybe his necktie?"

The mention of the word "necktie" jerked me back to reality. "Ugh, Cathie, there's a killer on the loose."

She sighed. "There always is."

"My former partner."

"George, right? I've met him. Awful guy."

"You're not kidding."

"He'd never bake and frost cupcakes and have them delivered to your office. Or send you three dozen purple irises."

"Correct, but irrelevant."

"Patrick kicked me out of my own kitchen," Cathie mused, "and obsessed over cupcakes. And buttercream frosting! He made *six batches* of buttercream frosting, one for each color."

"They were delicious."

"I don't like where this is going one bit. I can't see my brother as a wooing-lover type. I prefer him as a distant millionaire who uncomplainingly supports my parents and stays the hell out of my way."

"Mmmm?"

"And now he's moving here!"

"Yup."

"What do you have to say for yourself?"

"I need lunch if I'm going to have the energy to stop the bad guy. I gotta go."

"I hate you." She didn't sound convinced, or convincing. "Killer on the loose? *You're* the killer on the loose. You keep those legs closed until you put a ring on my brother's finger. Make him an honest man."

"If you don't stop talking, I'm going to videotape our first time and send it to you. That'll send you back to MIMH."

I heard the unmistakable sound of a raspberry and then she was off the line.

Chapter Eighty

When I got back from lunch I got word to go straight to Dr. Nessman's office. So much for my perfect day. I supposed I knew what was coming and had to admit I wasn't looking forward to it. Not least because the good doctor was right. He had been proven right all week.

His assistant, Karen, was on the phone and waved me in. I tried to brace myself for the pony onslaught, rapped lightly, and walked in.

"Hello, Cadence."

Ponies. Ponies *everywhere*. Posters. Pictures. Horse head bookends. And a horseshoe nailed to the top of the doorway! (Dr. Nessman thought it was lucky, which just goes to show that psychiatrists are perfectly capable of going crazy right along with their patients.)

"Hi, Dr. Nessman."

"Hello. I don't suppose they've found Special Agent Pinkman yet?"

"Not yet." I plunked down into the chair opposite him. "The guy knows our tactics, so it may take a while."

Dr. Nessman shook his head, smiling a little. "And you know *his* tactics. No, with you on the case, I wouldn't want to be George Pinkman right now."

"No. You wouldn't."

"Fair enough." Nessman stared down at what I assumed was my file, or possibly the Chicago Yellow Pages. "Cadence, let's talk about all the shifting."

Shifting. Losing time. Coming forward. Going back. All words that meant the same thing: Shiro and Adrienne were coming out much more often, and I had no control at all. Not that I ever did.

"Okay," I said, except it wasn't. "What about it?"

"I think the longer you resist facing what happened to you as a child, the more difficult it will be for you to get well."

"But *I* won't be well at all. I'll just be an amalgam of Shiro and Adrienne and me. You can't have it both ways, right?"

"As I said in our earlier session," he said quietly, looking at me over the top of his glasses, "you were once a whole person. The state you are in now is a direct result of unendurable, inescapable stress placed on you during your formative years."

"Dr. Nessman, I know all this."

"And you're quite right. If you can ever be a whole person again, there would be a blending. But consider the alternative—what if Shiro dedides to become the dominant personality? Or Adrienne? They both have the power to shunt you aside and drive your body wherever they wish. What if they put you aside permanently?"

"They wouldn't, though," I said, shifting uneasily.

"To save themselves? To put you out of their way? Of course they would."

"Dr. Nessman, I've kind of got a lot on my plate right now. Can't we talk about this another time?"

"Cadence. Avoiding the discussion won't make the issue itself go away."

"I'll bet you got that from a fortune cookie."

"Teasing me won't work, either."

Maybe Tasering? I squirmed in my chair, feeling cornered. Dr. Nessman had the patience of a rock, so I couldn't outwait him. And he reported directly to Michaela, which meant he could recommend my suspension or even my termination, and chances were high that Michaela would take his advice. Well, on suspension, anyway. And I needed the money if I was going to buy a digital videocamera capable of holding and editing enough "brotherly love" sex scenes to send Cathie back to MIMH.

I was a worm on a hook, all right. And I could see that the only way to get out of this was to make a concession.

"You want to play *Let's Make a Deal*?"

Nessman arched an eyebrow at me. "What did you have in mind?"

"We can talk about my parents right now. We can talk about them every session for the next month if you want. The next six months. But then you have to shelve this whole integration thing for the same six months."

"Done," Dr. Nessman said so quickly that I cursed under my breath. Clearly, I had lowballed myself.

Chapter Eighty-one

"All right, Cadence, you're feeling relaxed. You're not sleepy; you're quite aware of what's going on. You're watching the light and you can hear me very well. Watching the light. All of your concentration is fixed on my voice and on the light. It's very calm and restful. Watching the light.

"Now we're going back, Cadence. We're going back but we won't really be there. We're just looking at the last time you saw your mother and father. But we're safe, Cadence. What we're seeing can't hurt us. It's like you're watching a movie. You can report what's happening while being in no danger at all.

"From your house, you can see the grounds of the hospital where you were born. The big rolling grass hills. The hospital itself. You are three. Your father is doing his best to take care of you. You live with him in the small red house on the west edge of the property that is his home as the custodian."

"He's mean."

"Yes. But he can't hurt you. Any of you. You're just watching a movie, Cadence."

"Mama's here."

"Wait for me, Cadence. Yes. Your mother is there. She's a patient. As we watch the film you remember that your father almost went to jail when the hospital administration realized your mother was pregnant by him."

"He was mean. He made her."

"Yes. But once you were born your mother adored you. She never blamed you for the details of your conception. By your first birthday she was very happy that she could see you every day."

"He tricked them."

"Yes, he did. He managed to fool almost everyone—he fooled them into thinking he could be a good man and a good father."

"But not Mama."

"No. Your mother never quite trusted him after you were conceived, but she was willing to set that aside to visit you."

"She's not taking the medicine."

"That's right, Cadence. She thought she could be a better mother if she went off her meds. She wanted to keep a close eye on your father. And your mother was a veteran of state hospitals. She knew how to make the staff think she was taking her meds. She was very, very smart and she was happy to risk her health and her sanity and her life if she thought it would make her a better mother.

"Cadence, it's the day after your third birthday. The date is September 20, and the hospital grounds are covered with—"

"Rainbow leaves."

"Yes, there are beautiful leaves all over the grounds. It's your father's job to clean them up. He's—"

"No."

"We're just watching a movie. Nothing can hurt you while we watch the movie.

"Now your mother comes to the small red house you share with your father; she is bringing a small—"

"It's pink."

"Yes, a small cake with pink frosting. She's bringing it to you but your father is angry."

"He forgot. He was mad because he forgot my birthday, but she remembered."

"Yes. And that's when the geese come."

"No it's not."

"Yes, Cadence. It's autumn and they're fattening themselves up for the long flight south. They are beautiful Canada geese. There are dozens roaming all over the grounds. They are nearly tame; you can walk right up to them and feed them."

"He's mad. But he's pretending he's not. He's pretending to make a joke."

"That's right. And as your mother approaches—"

"Don't come over here, Mama!"

"Shhhh, shhhh, we're just watching. Your mother is coming and your father swerves his small tractor lawn mower. But he isn't aiming for your mother, he's—"

"The goose."

"That's right. And you can hear what he's saying. He's saying—"

"Watch this."

"Yes. And the goose doesn't have enough time to fly away. So—"

"He runned it over! It couldn't get away and he runned right over it! And I'm—"

"You're not there, Cadence. You are a grown woman, not that toddler. You're only watching what the three-year-old is doing."

"—screaming, I'm screaming and Mama's screaming oh she's so *mad*."

"Yes. She saw your father scare the three-year-old on purpose. She has been off her meds for over a month. She is angry at the terror she sees on her child's face. She—"

"The cake. Pink. It's pink."

"Yes. She throws the cake at him. He tries to duck and one of his hands leaves the wheel. He's off balance."

"Mama knocked him down."

"That's right. She was able to surprise him, and knock him off the small tractor. And then, in an attempt to protect you and avenge herself, she—"

"She runned over him. Like he runned over the goose. Stop screaming! Nobody can *think* if you don't stop screaming!"

"You're not screaming, Cadence. You're watching. You're seeing your father injured at first."

"Just his arm, the first time."

"Did he get angry?"

"Oh yes. That's when Mama and him start fighting for real. He gets up with one arm and reaches for her throat. She knocks him back. He looks over at me and comes for me. He blames me. My cake. My mother. He'll take care of her, by taking care of me."

"He's looking for someone he can defeat. He can't defeat her."

"No one can. Especially not on a mower. First she knocks him down with a tree branch. He doesn't move much, even when she gets back on the tractor . . . and she . . . and she . . ."

"She finishes the job. And the three-year-old, she saw it all. The birthday girl saw it all, saw the fighting, saw the father's calculated cruelty, saw your mother help you in the only way she could think of. But it's too much, Cadence. For the birthday girl."

"I don't—I don't know where I'm going."

"That's right, Cadence. In a minute, the movie won't pick up for another seven months. Because Adrienne is being born. Adrienne does what the birthday girl could not—she screams and she yells and she cries and she hurts anyone who gets too close. And also during those months—"

"Shiro comes."

"Yes. If Adrienne's job is to help the birthday girl have an outlet for her rage, then Shiro's job is to remember. And to fight. To keep the birthday girl safe. It is the last time you were ever a whole person."

"I told him! I told him to watch out for the goose and he *didn't*! And then Mama runned over him and—and—"

"And when the birthday girl came back that spring, her mother was dead also."

"She wanted to fly. Like the geese."

"Yes. She was facing a lifetime of punishment for what she did. Worst of all, she would never see her daughter again. She managed to get to a roof without anyone stopping her and then leapt to her death. Shiro saw this; the birthday girl never did. Adrienne is your outlet for fear; Shiro is your memory. Shiro remembers *everything.*"

Chapter Eighty-two

"I do not want to be."

"I know, Shiro."

"I wish I did not."

"Yes, that's right."

"I do not *want* to be the birthday girl's memory. I do not want to remember anything. But there is no way to escape. Even if I try not to look, I can still see. I see everything. I see the girl and the goose and the leaves and Daddy all red on the ground."

"Yes. But I am speaking with Cadence right now. Your task is to watch and listen. So Cadence will come back out in five seconds. But thank you, Shiro. Thank you for allowing Cadence to see into your earliest memory."

"No."

"This is Cadence's time, Shiro. You will all have your turn."

"Do not send me away. The dark and the screaming never, ever stop."

"You're all safe here. Shiro, listen: five. Four. Three. Two. One."

Chapter Eighty-three

I was on my knees. I was on my knees and my face was wet. So were my fingers. I was—I had been crying. Was still crying. But Dr. Nessman was there. He was down on one knee beside me, making the girasol shine.

"She wasn't bad," I sobbed. I turned my hands over and saw with no surprise that there were four crescents on each palm, bloody crescents from Shiro clenching our fists. "She wasn't! She was just trying to give me a cake. Just trying to be a mom. Even when she rode him down on that tractor."

"Yes, Cadence." He handed me some Kleenex. "That's exactly right. Your mother did all she could, but in a way, what happened that September destroyed you all. Your family was never, ever the same. And neither were you. And you know something else now, don't you?"

I didn't say anything. But Nessman was kindly relentless. "Cadence?"

I took a deep breath and wiped my eyes. "It wasn't my

fault. His choice and her choice weren't my fault. I was just a little kid."

"That's right. You were a very young child and your third birthday is your first conscious memory. But it blew your psyche into pieces, and more than two decades later, you're still trying to finish the puzzle."

I was still on my knees. I blew my nose and dully observed that my hands were shaking. "She had red hair. My mother. She had red hair."

"Yes. You honored her at that time the only way you could—you invested Adrienne with your mother's crazy reckless courage, her coloring, even some of her personality. Adrienne is the monument you built to preserve the memory of your mother."

I cried harder. I couldn't seem to stop. Maybe that was going to be my new job. Crying all the time.

Oh, Mama.

Chapter Eighty-four

When I returned to work the next day, I don't think I was imagining it when people where a bit nicer to me. Pam, sporting pajamas with unicorns riding unicycles, had thoughtfully removed all appointments from my day. Beth swung by with a dozen different recipes for cakes and brownies—she didn't know I was dating a millionaire baker, the famous Aunt Jane. Frick and Frack were nowhere to be found.

Michaela took me out to lunch at a sushi restaurant, where she glared at the bar chef as he chopped tuna rolls and sliced salmon.

"Manhunt for George has gone nationwide," she informed me. "We've also advised border agents with Canada and Mexico of the risk he presents. TSA is also aware; but we don't think he'd try to fly anywhere."

"Not unless he could drive the plane," I agreed. I marked my sushi menu carefully: two orders nigiri hamachi, two orders sashimi sake. That and a miso soup would do me.

"We've got local law enforcement crawling all over his

house in Wayzata. Hasn't been back. I wish we knew where he was."

I shrugged. "He takes pride in being unpredictable. And of course, he knows our procedures. I imagine he's one or two states away, in a hotel in some suburban area where the staff aren't going to be looking for a killer. He'd have enough cash reserves to stay off the electronic grid; and using a cash deposit is still common enough that it's hard to look—"

Michaela's cell rang. "It's Pam." She flipped it open, listened, and flipped it closed.

"He's still in Minneapolis. A lone cop spotted him on Hennepin Avenue and tracked him for about half a block before losing him. We're putting a quiet cordon around the neighborhood."

"He could be trying to stay close so he can attack witnesses."

"Scherzo's closer, but North Minneapolis is still a ways off. Plus, neither witness really has much to offer anymore."

"George doesn't know that. In fact, he's proven it by attacking Jeremy once already. I'd feel more comfortable if you told me to go."

"Go, then. I'll find an agent to rendezvous with you. Then get to Ms. Carr. Get them both back to HQ and secure them for the next twenty-four hours. I'm heading to Hennepin with most everyone else."

Chapter Eighty-five

To my surprise and delight, I didn't have to find Tracy. She was with Jeremy.

"Agent Jones!"

I returned her smile. "I wasn't expecting to find you here. But I'm glad. Jeremy's here, too?"

He was. A simple bandage on the back of his shaved head was the only visible sign of the trauma he had suffered the last time I was there. I thought wistfully of the Dobermans, who had tried so hard to kill me.

"So you know each other?"

"Tj-tj-just recently. At your office."

"After you interviewed me, Jeremy was still hanging around," Tracy explained. "We've kinda hit it off. I hope that's okay?"

I shrugged. "You don't need federal permission to date in this country. At least not yet."

They giggled. "Dr-dr-Tracy and I spent some time talking to your janitor. Uh-uh-Opus. Nice guy."

"I think the proper term is 'custodian.'" Tracy was smiling, but it was thin and I could see that she didn't care for the topic of Opus. "Jeremy, I doubt Cadence cares much about all the staff we met at the office."

"No, I like Opus!"

"Yeah. He sz-sz-says he's pretty taken with you, too. I d-d-think he has a crush on you."

I searched Jeremy's face for any sign of cruelty or teasing, but saw none. Yeah, I guess Opus did seem sort of sweet on me. It irritated me that there were so few people at BOFFO who were nice enough to the guy for him to focus romantic energy on them. Sure, we were a cluster of freaks, perverts, obsessives, isolationists, and sociopaths. But we were federal employees! It was time to hold ourselves to a higher standard.

"Can I get you something to drink?" Tracy offered. "I think Jeremy has a beer or two in his fridge. I've had one already."

"No thanks." I turned and looked out the window, down the street. I could almost make out the liquor store Adrienne had broken into. But that's not where my mind was.

"Jeez, Trace. She's aw-aw-aw-on duty. Hey, I kt-kt-can get you a water if that's b-b-better."

I tried to keep my voice light. "Sounds super!" I was sweating in any case. It didn't help that I was standing right about where George's necktie had been.

Finding articles of clothing at a crime scene does not constitute airtight evidence that the owner did it.

Jeremy and Tracy had gotten awfully tight, awfully quickly. They shared a few attributes, to be sure: a "survival" experience with the ThreeFer Killer, some minor personality quirks, the ability to make it through an interview with a federal agent without giving much useful detail, and apparently a familiarity with the contents of Jeremy's refrigerator.

And now he's calling her "Trace" within twenty-four hours of allegedly meeting her, even though she's never offered it up as a nickname to me through two or three substantial and friendly conversations.

Didn't he say those dogs belonged to a sister? Wasn't she moving around? Didn't those dogs try to rip your throat out?

Ice crept up my spine. Hearing the water pour out of the kitchen faucet behind me made me want to pee. Bad.

The two of them had stopped the friendly conversation. They were watching me, I knew.

Has she figured it out? Is she going to break?

I couldn't turn around to face them. Terror was actually clogging my throat; in fact, terror felt an awful lot like cotton wads jammed past my tonsils. I couldn't move. I almost couldn't think. I didn't know—

Hang on, sister.

What?

I am coming. Right now. Just stand still. Try to smile. Say something sappy. Laugh if you can.

I said, "Boy, this neighborhood is beautiful!" then broke into a coughing fit.

I suppose you are doing the best you can, Shiro said from the side of my brain. *Relax. I am*

Chapter Eighty-six

Here. I was right here.

I took a deep, steadying breath to lose Cadence's cough. I could understand her terror; the last clues had dropped on her like cluster bombs.

Jeremy and Tracy were, of course, the ThreeFer Killers.

Things fell into place with near-sickening rapidity. Like any test question, once you knew the answer, everything else was obvious. The evidence was still circumstantial—but far stronger than it had been with George.

Tracy hadn't been a living victim—she was in on it. She had been planted. And while we were all looking the other way, her accomplice, Jeremy, was already in place making mischief and muddying the waters.

Were they siblings, as Jeremy's comment about the dogs suggested? Lovers? A killer team-up of murderers, like Bianchi and Buono, the Hillside Strangler? Or Carol Bundy and Doug Clark, the Sunset Strip Killer?

Time to mull over that later. For now, for this small spot of time, Tracy and Jeremy must not must not *must not* suspect I was driving the body. They would not understand this quirk in a federal agent and they would immediately become suspicious. They had to believe I was still Cadence: giddy and charming and not at all disturbed by their company, or much of anything else.

"—something to eat?"

Eh? Ah. Jeremy, doubtless trying to trick me into ingesting something that would make me sleep, so he and Trace could drag me—us—to some fetid alley where he could cut our throats and then draw things with our blood.

Keep underestimating me, Jeremy. "I would rather—uh—that, that—yeah, that would be super fantastic neato!" I tried to sound as enthusiastic as a cheerleader cheering for—er—whatever it was in sports a cheerleader cheered for. "Just golly—gadget cool!"

"Jeremy just offered to make steaks for me," Tracy suggested. "You like steaks, right?"

"Absolutely niftilicious! Jeepers, that sounds tasty." If I had to keep this up much longer, I was going to need an insulin shot. "Ah, but here's the problem: I have got—ahem, I gotta get you guys outta here, stat! My boss will be soooo mad at me if you get yourselves killed and all. You know, because we stayed here. With the ThreeFer Killer."

They looked at each other.

"You know, George Pinkman! He's, ah, still at large. Still walkin' around out there." It felt good to inject as much truth as I could into this charade. "Cop just spotted him on Hennepin less than an hour ago. Guy could be on the way here. So this isn't safe." I circled the kitchen with my fingers. "Nothing here is safe. We gotta get all out of here and stuff."

Jeremy shrugged. "Okay. To where?"

"Why, HQ, silly! It is, *gah* it's, the only place to be!" I tried to laugh, feeling ridiculous. How could I look anything like Cadence? We looked different, dressed different, talked different, acted different . . . there was no way they were buying this.

He looked at Tracy, who smiled weakly and nodded, and then he turned back to me. "Lead the way, Agent Jones."

I wondered if he realized he was no longer stuttering. I sincerely hoped he wasn't fucking with me as I was with him.

I made my eyes widen to better imitate Cadence's big-eyed deer-in-the-headlights stare. "Well, sure! Sure, sure! You want to ride with me instead of in your own car, and that only makes sense, cuz y'know, for your protection." *Fuck*. How was I going to alert anyone with them always two feet away? And what if they were armed? "That is just a Brillo-shiny idea, and it will also save on gas and protect the environment, which is one of my many duties as a socially and environmentally conscious member of our society." Hmmm. That came out a little stilted. I added, "So it'll be superawesome and fun! And awesome. But mostly fun! Let's saddle up, tiny soldiers!"

I was giving myself a migraine. I should be getting some sort of award for this . . . an Oscar, or possibly the Nobel Peace Prize.

What to do? Call for backup? I had no proof, only Cadence's hunch. But I wasn't about to get in a car and go off with them unless a SWAT team knew all about it. And possibly the marines. I was a good fighter, but these two psychotics had killed more than a dozen people in less than two years—and they had done it without anyone figuring out anything, until today.

If they had stayed gone, we would probably never have caught them. But like all Bond-influenced villains, they had to put themselves in harm's way to prove how clever they were.

Well, it was my job to make them pay for that mistake. Without making any dumb mistakes of my own. BOFFO was counting on me. Society was counting on me.

My sisters were counting on me.

"Let's get to that car then!"

Chapter Eighty-seven

Texting would be too suspicious in front of them, but a quick call to Michaela would work, right? I called on our way out to the car.

"Do you have Jeremy, Cadence?" she asked. "Is he safe?"

"Oh, he is *more* than safe, boss." I gave Jeremy the thumbs-up and a smile. "He's *super*safe! You don't get safer than that. And Tracy's here, too. That's right, she was here the whole time. It was convenientastic!"

"Are you all right, Cadence?"

I took a chance that my charges could not hear the other end of the line. "No! Not at all! And we are heading back to HQ right now." *Please, Michaela. Put it together.*

"All right. I know you're stressed out, but do what you can. Make them comfortable and make sure they're not too distressed. We don't need a lawsuit right now."

"Say, have you found George yet?" I got into the car as Tracy got into the passenger seat and Jeremy got in behind me.

"Obviously not."

"No, of course not. Gosh, he's a devil to find. I wonder if we ever will. The guy could be dead, for all we know." This was as far as I dared go.

"I doubt it. But I am beginning to suspect that the sighting was a false alarm. We won't be too far behind you, Agent Jones. An hour or two at best."

"Anyone back at the office who can help me through the secured-witness process?"

"Agent Jones, they've already been through that process."

Sigh. "So, just Pam then."

"Just Pam then. And probably Opus."

I did some quick math in my head. Three of us, two of them. Only one of us was a trained agent.

Not quite fifty-fifty.

But there was nowhere else to go.

"See you back at the office, then. Don't forget our meeting in thirty minutes!"

"Agent, there is no—"

I hung up, taking a mental note to train my boss on how to spot stress in a colleague's phone manner. Sure, it would not be as fun as whittling phallic objects; but surely she would see the point after today.

Chapter Eighty-eight

I felt a bit safer now that Jeremy and Tracy knew I had called in and reported my status—and the fact that they were with me. Surely, self-preservation would keep them smart.

Indeed, we made it to BOFFO headquarters without Tracy accusing me of being onto them, or Jeremy attempting to garrote me with a George Pinkman necktie. I took them through the automated security portals—ruing the fact that there were only two security guards in our office who could assist me with this matter. Naturally, we ran into neither of them.

"Anyone here?" I called out. I'd been around BOFFO when it was empty, to be sure. This was creepier than that. "Pam? Opus? Hello?"

"I'll ba-ba-bet they're in your conference room," Jeremy guessed.

"Why do you say that?"

He held up a cell phone. "I sent a mi-mi-message ahead for them to be there. While in the car. Sh-sh-seemed you were onto us."

Them? My heart sank. Whatever math I had figured out, these two had outcalculated.

Sure enough, by the time we made it to the conference room, there were two figures securely cuffed and facedown on the floor. Pam was one of them. Poor agoraphobic thing was streaming tears—even here in a confined space, trouble had come to her.

Next to her was . . . George Pinkman! He looked furious.

Looming above them both was the hulking form of whom I now understood to be the third party in the ThreeFer killing conspiracy: Cadence's good janitor friend Opus.

Chapter Eighty-nine

I was startled to find myself back at BOFFO headquarters, and certainly not happy to see my good buddy Opus as a bad guy in cahoots with Tracy and Jeremy. I was even more distressed when I saw Pam crying.

George sputtering on the floor—I guess I didn't mind that too much. Though he smelled like he had pooped his pants.

Why did Shiro leave me here? It couldn't just be to enjoy George messing himself. This is a dangerous situation.

And one that requires thought.

Delegation, I finally guessed glumly. *Shiro wants me to sweet-talk Opus. She and Adrienne get all the fun jobs. I get the work.*

He didn't look angry or mean, to be sure. Just very, very large.

"Opus. I'm disappointed to see you here."

He cocked his head. "Cadence?"

"It may still be Shiro," Tracy pointed out. This knocked me back a step: *They know my secret? My names?*

Of course they knew my names. With Opus on the inside, they probably had full files on me.

I took a deep breath. "Yes. Cadence. Opus, why would you do this? I thought we were friends."

He nodded. "We're friends."

"My friends don't cuff people and shove them onto the floor and scare them until they cry," I pointed out. I looked down. "Well. Maybe George."

"Fuck you, Jones! Get me the fuck out of here!"

"Michaela will be happy I found you."

"Christ, all you people had to do was look in the goddamn broom closet! I've been there for days. I had to crap my own pants in there; you couldn't follow the smell?"

Opus lifted a bottle of Citrus Windex, pointed it downward, and spritzed the back of George's messy suit pants. "Stay quiet. I'm talking to Cadence. Cadence is nice. Cadence doesn't like you much. Not when you call me rain man."

"Fuck you, you crazy retard, you fucking rain man, you fucking retarded rain man! I'm going to fuck you up when I get up!"

"George, please shut up. I'm getting a handle on this."

"Nice fucking handle, triple bitch—"

Opus kicked him in the head, and his lights went out. I opened my mouth to protest, but thought better of it. "Opus, that was sweet. You're right. I don't like George much. But Pam's my friend. Look at her. She's terrified. She's not a trained agent. Did you have to do that to her?"

Opus motioned to Jeremy but wouldn't look at any of us. "Brother told me to. Brother said I had to. Everyone in cuffs. That's what brother said."

"I did," Jeremy agreed. I looked for the family resemblance. It was hard, since Opus was so shaggy and large, and Jeremy was smaller and had a shaved head. But I supposed I could see it.

"Opus was the large man I saw leaving your house. He left George's tie there."

"You can uncuff dt-dt-the secretary, Opus."

"She sits in that chair and doesn't move," Tracy added, pointing.

Pam dutifully went to the chair, but huddled in it with her knees over her face. What this was doing to her sense of BOFFO's office as a safe place I could only guess.

I decided to press my luck. "Why not let her go? We can leave the office before she could call anyone for help. They're all still—"

"No. We will only be a moment to make our proposal, and then you will have a decision to make, and then my brothers and I will either kill all three of you . . . or we won't."

Proposal? This was the oddest serial killing I'd ever been involved in.

Tracy motioned for me to sit down across from her. "So you know about the three of us now."

"You're triplets," I deduced. "You're close in age, and seeing you stand here together, it's easier to see some physical resemblance."

"Born v-v-five minutes apart."

"And of course you have . . . social eccentricities . . . that probably were a burden to you growing up."

"Burden." Tracy swallowed.

"Wa-wa-worse than burden," Jeremy added. "But we dj-dj-don't have time for a full counseling session today. We grew up close. Sh-sh-stayed close. Fought together. B-b-protected one another. Like you."

I looked at each of the three of them. They were not looking at me with anger, or hatred, or fear, or even calm murderous intent.

They were looking at me with admiration.

Opus took a step forward. "I found the nice agent at BOFFO. She was nice to me. I told the others: she can show us how she does it. She can show us how to fit in. She can show us. She can show us how to make it stop. Make it stop."

Tracy massaged her hands. "Make the proposal, Jeremy. Make her see. Time is running out."

"The others want m-m-me to talk," Jeremy explained with an apologetic, almost charismatic smile.

"That seems kind of mean."

"I don't mind stuttering," he managed without any tic at all. "And I find I can be persuasive."

"Your stutter's getting better."

"I'm closer to the apex."

"You mean the kill?"

"Maybe not this time. Maybe this time, it can be d-d-different." He grimaced. "Different."

I looked over at Tracy. "I don't understand. Say what you have to say."

"We want in."

"In? In to what?"

Tracy clicked her tongue impatiently. "In to *you*. Your life. Your work. What you do. Who you are."

"You want to *work* with me?"

"I work with you," Opus pointed out.

"Yes you do." I didn't know what else to say.

"And live with you," Jeremy rushed to add. I don't know what compelled him to think this would sweeten the offer. "Cadence, surely you see the symmetry of it all. What my siblings and I do together . . . what your siblings and you do together . . ."

"Is completely different," I finished for him.

Tracy hissed and I heard Opus whimper worriedly behind me—I couldn't help but feel a pang for my work buddy, even if he was one-third of a psychotic serial-killing mastermind team—but Jeremy instead sat down right next to me and put his hand over mine.

"You mo-mo-must see the symmetry, Cadence. The symmetry."

"Yeah, yeah, I see: three of this, three of that. Very clever. But that's—"

"That's *not* all," he interrupted angrily. "You're not paying attention! We complete you. Opus validates your need for true and meaningful companionship. Tracy validates your first sister's need for focus and proper planning. And I validate your second sister's need for . . ." He paused.

"Mayhem?" I offered.

"Unstructured expression."

"You believe I need these things."

"We believe you do. We believe BOFFO does. It makes so much sense, Cadence. Think about it. We know if you think about it, if you try hard enough, if you really want to help us and your friends, you will agree."

That was quite the string of nonstuttering—and Jeremy didn't say any more. I sensed the final offer was on the table.

I spoke slowly. "So let me understand: if I agree to help you get jobs here . . . and if I agree to live with you, so we can be together . . . you'll let Pam and George go?"

Jeremy bit his lip. Tracy leaned forward and stared at my sleeves. Opus looked everywhere in the room but at people.

I thought about these three—about Jeremy and Tracy in witness rooms, and Opus cleaning floors. I thought about the crime scenes they had left behind, and the bodies propped up and arranged carefully for me to notice clues. I thought about what they wanted from me personally, and how different that was from what Patrick wanted. I thought about the fact that they were in a rush . . . and that for all the masterful planning they (really, Tracy) had done and all the patient work they (really, Opus) had done to get this offer in front of me on their (really, Jeremy's) terms, they couldn't see the fatal flaw in their plan:

Murderers make for really superbad housemates and coworkers.

Also . . . sleep with these guys? *Ish.*

My traitorous mouth dropped open and I said, "Sleep with all of you?"

"Nuh-no!"

Oh. Because *that* would be really crazy.

"I—I just want a best friend. Like you have. They're the ones . . ." Tracy jerked a thumb at her brothers. "Well, you know."

Ah. Okay, slightly less nauseating. Trouble was, I already had a best girlfriend. I had caught my limit.

I stood and clapped my hands once. "Hey, guys, I know I should probably try to play along and give you false hope long enough for my fellow agents to show up and rescue me, but I don't do dishonest very well. So let me say: this is the most *fucked-up* idea I've ever heard!"

Wow, it felt good to swear.

When Jeremy rose and slugged me, it felt not nearly so good. But I was smiling, because I knew who was

Chapter Ninety

Coming to a fistfight near you!
Saturday
            Saturday!
                        SATURDAY!
She takes a punch!
      She doesn't
            (ever)
                        go down!
Ladies and
            Fuck the gentlemen
Let me introduce to you our contestants this evening.
In this corner
And that one
And the other one
We have our challengers
Some truly fucked-up
                  (geese)

motherfuckers who can't stop killing
and apparently can only count
To three.
(Boooooooooo!)
(Hissssssss!)
AAAAAAAAND in this corner—
The reeeeeeeigning champion!
(Raaaahhhh!)
(Yeeeeaaaa!)
The Super-Fed with the Triple Head!
The Lone Detective with All Perspective!
The Power Saw Who Plays the Law
AND SMACKS Y-Y-YOUR
LOWER J-J-JAW
F-F-FREAK
(Sleep tight.)
AAAAAAAAAAADRIEEEEEEEEEEENE
(Yo Adrienne!)
JOOOOOONES
That woman looks scared over there.
She must be
(a goose?)
(my daughter?)
(the guy under the lawn mower?)
MY NEXT VICTIM

Come here lady don't run away, don't run away from the lawn mower, there's no point, it will catch you and slice you like a goose

You'll be cooked

Oh stop running away this is pathetic
This is boring
WOW that hurt
What was that guy behind me swinging?
Some
Kind
Of
Lawn mower?
Nope. Just his fists.
Okay. Let's stick with this one. Let the woman go
POWWWWWWWWWWW that hurt
This guy is a house.
WHAM POW TAKE THAT KABLAM AND THAT SNAP-DAP RAPPADAP FLOAT LIKE A BUTTERFLY STING LIKE A
Why won't he GO DOWN
POWWWWWWWWWW that hurt too.
Getting nowhere.
Getting
(scared?)
bored.
Sister, come take care of this one.

Chapter Ninety-one

I cannot say I was completely thrilled when Adrienne turned things over to me. Granted, she had knocked Jeremy unconscious and chased Tracy out of the room altogether. But this still left Opus, who was very large, very strong . . .

. . . and not even dented by what Adrienne had thrown at him.

I ducked in time to miss the latest blow. What would probably "bore" Adrienne would no doubt knock me out. I was not going to win a slugging match with this man. No, the best I could hope for was . . .

"Pam, get me out of these fucking cuffs!"

George was awake again, flopping like an outraged trout.

"Damn it, Pam, why'd they let *you* go and not me! It's not fair! Get a cuff key from Shiro here and let me out. No, Pam—don't leave me in here with them! I can't defend—Pam! FUCKING PAJAMA-WEARING SLUT!"

I was glad to see Pam escape from the room. She would be bright enough to call for help.

So we would play the waiting game.

And the best one to get Opus to wait was

Chapter Ninety-two

"Cadence?"

I looked at Opus, this bear of a man with his fist still held up in the air, who recognized me the moment I showed up. I didn't have to say or do anything: he knew me. He could count the pieces of me and add them together faster than he could a carton of nails. It broke my heart.

"Oh, Opus . . ."

He lowered his fist. "You're not going to help us."

"I'm sorry, Opus."

"No. You aren't."

"I am, though. It's too bad we three can't live happily ever after with you three. I guess the complete arrogance of assuming I'd leap at the chance to get two lovers and a new best friend isn't a big deal, huh?"

Opus said nothing.

"I'm not the one who can help you, anyway. It's going to have to be someone else."

"There is no one else. No one else to help. We asked for

help we ASKED for help but that's when they said no. They said no, Cadence. They said no and the killing started. That started the killing and I'm TIRED of the killing, Cadence. There's no one to stop it. Stop it, Cadence, stop it!"

How about if you stop shouting, Opus, how about that?

He put his huge, meaty hands over his ears, dropped to his knees, and began to scream.

I did the only thing I knew how to do. I rushed to him and held him.

(Hey, if my sisters had wanted a more decisive solution, they should have stuck around.)

We stayed like that for some time—I don't know how long, really—until I heard my boss's voice behind me.

"Cadence. Step away from him."

I turned my head and saw Michaela, backed up by every agent and security guard we had—something like two dozen altogether.

I looked around the room. Jeremy was gone. George was still cuffed, but had rolled under the table and stopped speaking. His face was turned away from everyone. He was humiliated and quiet. Nothing had gone right for him here. I almost felt bad for him.

Not as bad as I felt for Opus, though.

"He's surrendering peacefully," I reminded Michaela. I felt this might be necessary, as she was brandishing a butcher's knife.

Opus whimpered and hung his head. His beefy arms flopped uselessly at his sides. Even if he could take on the entirety of BOFFO—and I didn't doubt he could give us a run for our money—there was no fight left in him.

"Opus. Pam tells me you hurt her."

"Brother told me. Brother told me to cuff everyone. Everyone in cuffs. Pam in cuffs. George in cuffs. Brother told me."

"Where is Jeremy?" I asked.

Michaela kept her focus on Opus. "Your brother is gone, Opus. He has apparently fled the scene. So has your sister. Do you understand, Opus? They've *left you behind.* They've left you. They made you hurt Pam and they left you."

"They wouldn't leave me! Sister has a plan. Sister always has a plan. She says it'll be okay. We'll be with Agent Jones soon. She'll be with Shiro. Brother'll be with Adrienne. I'll be with Cadence. Sister has a plan. It'll be okay. Cadence is here. Tell her, Cadence."

"I'm here, Opus." I didn't see the point of breaking his heart further.

Apparently, Michaela was not on the same tender page I was on. "Cadence has nothing more to say to you, Opus. You hurt her friend Pam. Do you know where Pam is right now, Opus? Can you guess?"

He kept staring at the floor. "Pam in the nice clean pajamas. Likes the floor to be superclean. Sleeps on the superclean floor. Clean floor means a clean sleeping bag. Clean sleeping bag means clean pajamas. Clean pajamas means clean Pam. Clean Pam means safe Pam. Pam stays in the office. Things are clean. Floor is clean."

"Yes, well, right now Pam is huddled on the very clean floor immediately under her desk, and she will not come out for anyone. Not even me. She keeps whispering into her cell phone. She called me, you see, and got me here. But now that I'm here, she still doesn't feel safe. She's still whispering into that phone.

It's the only thing she'll talk to. Even if I get under the desk with her, she won't acknowledge me."

Michaela stepped forward, and I realized I had to get out of the way. NOW.

Before Opus could react, she had the knife in his groin. He screamed for half a second, and then the blade had cut his throat.

He slumped to the floor, thudding like a gorilla carcass.

Michaela walked away. The agents dispersed. Someone came in and dragged George away. I stayed at Opus's side and wept as his blood seeped into the cheap gray

Chapter Ninety-three

carpet was getting wet. I did not intend to stay long.

"Opus," I said, slapping him on the cheek. His eyes were still open, and his pupils rolled slightly to take me in. He had no more than five or six seconds left.

"Cadence forgives you," I told him. "But I do not. And I will hunt down your sister, and your brother. Because they are murderers. Just like you."

He tried to say something, but he died instead.

Epilogue: The First

So Opus died, and the others fled. I guess what surprised me most, though, was that I didn't hate them. Don't get me wrong, I wanted to catch them—and would, darn it. Oh yes, you betcha.

But as frightening as they were, they were pitiable as well. At least I was coming to understand the causes and complications of my multiple personality disorder, and even that had taken over two decades for me to even begin to face.

The triplets had never had a chance.

Patrick is indeed hanging around, putting truth to Cathie's fears. He's still house hunting and we're having dinner tomorrow. At least, I think we are. I intend to keep my clothes on this time; but who knows?

Shiro or Adrienne might crash that party, and for the first time in my life, the thought doesn't fill me with horrified embarrassment. They're just as much a part of me as my hair and eye color. They look after me like my mother tried to—and I'm not going to disrespect that, or them.

But I swear. I swear on—on—on whatever. If Shiro sticks *one more cigarette* into my mouth . . .

Well. I guess some threats are best left vague.

Epilogue: The Second

Some threats are best left vague? That sounds like a complete lack of imagination to me—not to mention a lack of commitment.

And as a matter of fact, Patrick has asked *me* out for breakfast tomorrow. Cadence might pretend not to mind if I crash her party—but I will certainly mind if she crashes mine.

I am dismayed about Opus. Cadence has it right when she figures the triplets had never had a chance. And she is right when she realizes that *we* had. Those who ignore history are condemned to repeat it—and as far as I am concerned, my sisters and I do not plan to repeat anything.

Do yourselves a favor, Tracy and Jeremy.

Stay lost.

Epilogue: The Third

First comes the Opus
And then comes the
First comes the Tracy
And then comes the
Stutter, then comes the stuttering screams,
all stuttering screams
(he misses his Opus)
then comes the screams, and
The wheels on the bus go round and round,
Round and round,
Patrick's so brave.
I just want to see,
I just want to look at him
(and save him he is so silly he
thinks I I I need saving! Ha! Ha-ha!
Silly Pillsbury Doughboy!)

And I just want to hurt
Make them bleed

Tracy and Jeremy hurt
They hurt everyone
Their love is poison and we are the flowers
They try to kill
Kill with their love
The garden is not safe was never ever safe the flowers are dying and here come the geese.
Allll daaaaay lonnnnng.

They had better they had better they
They should they should
Stay away.
and disappear,
Disappear
Disappear
Good-bye, Opus! You shouldn't have
Shouldn't have
You should have left Cadence alone.
You should have left us alone.
How do you like being alone? Are you cold in the earth, Opus? Is it wet down there, and damp, and muddy?
Yes yes!
It is.
Warned you.
Won't warn you again. Do you want company down there in the dark, Opus? Do you do you

Do you?

Make them keep away. Make them. Make them.

Or I will

I will

IIIIIIII will.

And you won't be lonesome

And you won't be cold

But you'll be dead like Mommy dead like Daddy

Dead dead dead

Round and round.

All day long.